Ernst Klett Sprachen
Stuttgart

1. Auflage 1 7 6 5 4 3 | 2027 26 25 24 23

Alle Drucke dieser Auflage sind unverändert und können im Unterricht nebeneinander verwendet werden. Die letzte Zahl bezeichnet das Jahr des Druckes.
www.klett-sprachen.de

Herausgeber: Peter Bruck
Redaktion: Paul Newcomb
Layoutkonzeption: Elmar Feuerbach
Gestaltung und Satz: Joachim Schrimm, bostext, Friolzheim
Umschlaggestaltung: Maja Merz
Titelbild: Getty Images, phillipspears, München
Druck und Bindung: Medienhaus Plump GmbH, Rheinbreitbach

Printed in Germany

ISBN 978-3-12-577282-3

9 783125 772823

Contents

Abbreviations used in the annotations

abb	abbreviation
adj	adjective
AE	American English
e.g.	for example
esp	especially
etc	et cetera
Fr	French
idm	idiom
i.e.	that is
inf	informal
n	noun
off	offensive
opp of	opposite of
os	oneself
pl	plural
sb	somebody
sl	slang (be careful how you use it!)
sth	something
usu	usually

About the author

Todd Strasser was born on May 5, 1950 in New York City. After finishing high school, he attended New York University for a few years before dropping out. He then lived on a commune for a while and spent time in Europe, where he was a street musician. After returning to the US, he went to Beloit College to study literature and creative writing.

After this he worked for a newspaper and later at an advertising agency. In 1978 he sold his first novel, *Angel Dust Blues,* which depicts a 17-year-old boy who is neglected by his rich parents and becomes involved in drug dealing. From the money he received from the sales of this book, he started a fortune cookie company and for the next 12 years he sold more cookies than books.

Todd Strasser is the author of more than 140 books for young adults and teens. They have been translated into more than a dozen languages, and several have been adapted into feature films. In Germany he is best known for his *The Wave,* which he published under the pen name Morton Rhue.

He has also written for television, newspapers, and magazines such as *The New Yorker, Esquire* and *The New York Times.*

His work is sometimes controversial; he has written about topical themes such as nuclear war, Nazism, bullying in schools, homelessness, and school shootings.

Strasser has received many awards for his work. For example, in 2015, *No Place* was awarded the status of *Notable Social Studies Trade Book For Young People* by The National Council for Social Studies.

Here are some more books by Todd Strasser: *Famous* (2011), *If I Grow Up* (2009), *Boot Camp* (2006), *Can't Get There from Here* (2004), *Give a Boy a Gun* (2000)

About the book

In 2008 a major recession hit the United States. Many families lost their jobs, their sense of security and in many cases their homes, too: they could no longer pay back the money they had borrowed from banks. Today more than 550,000 Americans experience homelessness on any given night.

The financial, social and mental effects of homelessness are explored in this novel. The narrator and main character – 17 year old Dan Halprin – is a middle class teenager who had never imagined that he and his parents would ever have to give up their comfortable life.

For Dan moving to Dignityville is just the beginning of his problems. He experiences embarrassment, shame and humiliation even though his friends are sympathetic to his new condition. However, the changes in his life are dramatic: he can no longer afford to go out, do the things he used to do with his friends and his girlfriend Talia. As a result, he spends less time with her and more time with Meg, who also lives at Dignityville. But there are positive aspects of Dan's new life.

Local reaction to Dignityville and its inhabitants is also important in *No Place*. Dan Halprin's story is one that affects all of society.

Dan dreams of having a professional baseball career that would make him enough money to support his parents. Find out on your own if the novel has a Hollywood-like happy ending…

To Fred and Glen,
who've been there for so long. Thanks, guys.

PROLOGUE

In the dark I'm jogging quickly across the hospital parking lot toward the emergency room. My cell phone vibrates. Even before I dig it out of my pocket, I know it's Talia and she's going to ask why I'm not at the party.

I answer with a lie: "Hey, sorry, the stupid bus hasn't come yet."

Silence on the other end. Talia's pondering this.

"I'll be there ASAP," I add as I weave through parked cars.

"You sound like you're running," she says.

"Yeah, I'm, uh, running over to the Gerson Street stop so I can get the 104 or the 107. See you soon, okay?" I hate lying, especially to people I care about, but when everything's going wrong, it's sometimes hard to do what's right.

As a damp gust of wind carries the promise of rain, leaves swirl in the heavy moist air. From the distance comes the rumble of thunder. I push through the ER doors and into the stark bright fluorescent world of the hospital.

"May I help you?" asks the nurse behind the desk.

"I'm looking for Aubrey Fine."

"Family?"

"Yes." *Another lie.*

She points toward a pair of double doors. "Through there. Number three."

A sign on the wall says:

PLEASE TURN OFF YOUR CELL PHONE

Mine's vibrating again. It's Talia, and I don't answer. I feel like a juggler with one too many balls in the air. Inside the ER the beds are hidden by blue privacy curtains and the air smells antiseptic. Through a part in some curtains I glimpse a wrinkled white-haired old lady with her eyes closed and a greenish clear

7 **to ponder sth** to think about sth carefully – 8 **ASAP** *(abb, inf)* as soon as possible – 15 **to swirl** [swɜːrl] to move around fast and in an approximate circle – 16 **ER** *(abb)* emergency room *(Notaufnahme)* – 29 **wrinkled** [ˈrɪŋklᵊd] *faltig*

mask on her face. Then I'm outside the curtain of number three. From within comes a hushed female voice: "It's too soon to tell. We have to get him stabilized first."

I part the curtains just enough to see the doctor in a white medical jacket. She has straight blond hair, wears dark-rimmed glasses, and holds a clipboard. Meg is leaning over the hospital bed, her face partly obscured by her thick, curly, reddish brown hair, the sleeves of her too-long plaid shirt hanging over the bars.

There's someone in the bed and my stomach knots when I realize it's Aubrey. Nearly unrecognizable, his head is bandaged, chin scraped and scabbed, nose bent, bloody, and twice its normal size, one eye dark and swollen shut. Clear plastic tubes snake into his nose and have been forced between his split and swollen lips. His left arm is bandaged in a way that makes me think it's broken.

What did they do to him?

The doctor sees me. "Can I help you?"

Meg looks up, eyes red-rimmed and bloodshot, cheeks streaked with tears, surprised. "Dan!"

"Yeah, I–"

"You know him?" the doctor asks. She's clearly a by-the-rulebook type.

"Yes." Meg's still staring at me. "How did you ...?"

"It was on the news." It's strange to hear myself say that. A few months ago I barely knew the news existed. Well, I knew, but I hardly cared. Now, not only do I care, but it feels like half the time I'm part of it.

Meg looks pale and scared. I'm glad I came; she shouldn't have to go through this alone. Her mom must be back at Dignityville looking after her father. The curtain slides open and two guys in blue scrubs come in and start to fiddle with the machines and tubes.

2 **hushed** very quiet – 8 **plaid** [plæd] *(AE) kariert* – 30 **Dignityville** fictitious name for a tent camp – 32 **scrubs** *(pl)* pants and T shirt worn by hospital staff

"We're taking him to the ICU now," the doctor says, gently, to Meg.

My guts twist when the guys in the scrubs arrange Aubrey's limp right arm and bandaged left. You can tell he's out cold. It's the first time I've ever seen a beating victim–the swollen dark bruises and patches of dried blood …

"Can I come?" Meg asks.

"Not yet," the doctor answers. Then to me: "Why don't you take her to the waiting room?" It may be posed as a question, but the firm look in her eyes implies that this is an order.

I take Meg's hand and lead her through the double doors. In the waiting room my phone vibrates again, and again I ignore it. In a red plastic chair, Meg falls apart, burying her face in my shoulder and shaking with sobs. Some people around the room stare, then turn away as if embarrassed for her.

"Coffee?" I ask a little later. Meg nods, and I head down a polished corridor looking for the hospital cafeteria. When I come back there's a woman with Meg. She has an iPad on her lap, is wearing a dark blue pants suit, and has kinky hair that starts out black on top and then changes to orange-red as if she dyed it months ago and is now letting it grow out. I hand Meg a coffee, some sugar packets, and a couple of little half-and-halfs.

"Friend?" the woman asks Meg.

Meg nods, sniffs, wipes fresh tears out of her eyes. "Dan, this is Detective … uh …"

"French." The woman offers her hand.

"Dan Halprin." We shake.

"I'm asking Meg some questions," Detective French says.

Sounds like she doesn't want me there. "Sure, no prob." I start to back away.

"Can't he stay?" Meg blurts anxiously.

1 **ICU** *(abb)* Intensive Care Unit – 29 **prob** *(sl, abb)* problem – 31 **to blurt** [blɜːrt] to utter suddenly

Detective French gives me a hard look, as if to let me know this is serious business and she's only allowing me there for Meg's sake. I sit, sip some coffee, look around. The waiting room is about a quarter full. A sad-looking little girl with pigtails leans into her mother, who's busy texting on her phone. A greasy-haired guy with a crutch and a foot wrapped in a dirty bandage stares into space. You get the feeling they're not emergencies–just people who can't afford a doctor or have no place else to go.

"Why was Aubrey in the parking lot behind Ruby's?" Detective French asks Meg.

"He's a bartender there."

"Did he have enemies at work? Did he ever mention anyone?"

Meg shakes her head. "No, never."

"What about robbery?" I ask.

Detective French looks at me with an expression that says I should stay out of this, but answers just the same. "He still had his wallet when the officers arrived. There was money in it." She swipes the screen of the iPad with her finger. "There was a witness. … The person who called 911 … she said she heard one of them say something about Dignityville?"

Meg looks down at her mud-colored coffee. "That's … where we live."

"But Ruby's is all the way on the other side of town." I can't help butting in again. "How would anyone *there* know he had anything to do with Dignityville?"

Detective French tilts her head as if to say, *Think about it.*

They had to know who Aubrey was ahead of time.

Which means the attack wasn't random.

"Was he in a gang?" Detective French asks Meg.

Meg raises her head, frowns. "What kind of gang?"

"Street gang?"

"No! Never."

"You're sure?" Detective French doesn't sound convinced.

24 **to butt in** to interrupt a conversation – 28 **random** by chance

"Yes!" Meg's eyes start to fill with tears of frustrated indignation. "Why would you ...?"

"They used the preferred gangbanger weapon, a baseball bat. And there were green and gold gang beads in the parking lot. The police think they broke during the fight."

Meg scowls. "Street gangs around here?"

"From Burlington," Detective French says.

Burlington's ten miles away.

I feel sick picturing Aubrey on the ground getting bashed with a baseball bat, flailing to protect himself, accidentally catching a strand of the attacker's beads with his fingers. But wait. "How do you know the beads were from the fight? Maybe someone dropped them weeks ago."

Detective French gives me an impatient look like she wishes I'd keep my mouth shut. But Meg cocks her head alertly as if she wants to know the answer too. The detective explains: "There was blood in the parking lot. The beads weren't under it. They were on it."

"So?" Meg asks with a puzzled expression.

"Like the cherry on top of a sundae?"

Thanks to the graphic description, Meg starts to cry again. I put my arm around her. Detective French closes her iPad, says she's sorry about what happened to Aubrey, and thanks Meg for her time. She stands up and hands me a card. "In case she thinks of anything, or just wants to talk."

Meg's sobs trickle into whimpers. The minutes creep past. A guy staggers in, assisted by a friend, his hand wrapped in a T-shirt bright red with blood. They're immediately sent through the double doors into the emergency room. Meanwhile the texting mother dispatches her little girl to get a bag of chips from the vending machine.

3 **gangbanger** *(AE, sl)* violent street gang – 4 **bead** [bi:d] small piece of metal, shaped like a ball, part of a necklace – 10 **to flail** [fleɪl] to throw his arms and hands around

Finally the blond doctor comes out. Meg and I get to our feet. The doctor looks grim. "His condition is critical. He's in a coma."

Meg gasps and grabs my hand for support.

"Everything depends on the next twenty-four hours. If we can get past that, the neurologists can run tests."

"So you don't even know if ...?" Meg trails off as if she can't speak the words.

The doctor shakes her head. "We'll know tomorrow. You should go home now."

"But. ..."

"There's nothing you can do here," the doctor repeats, and gives me the same commanding look as before. This time it says, *Take her home.*

I lead Meg outside. Rain pours down in a dull roar and we stand under the canopy, chilled by the cold, wet mist. Meg begins to cry again; I just want to get her back to Dignityville before anything else bad happens.

And my stupid phone won't stop vibrating.

PART ONE

1

TWO MONTHS AGO

It was never easy with Talia. The second you said something she didn't like, she had five different ways of letting you know. Since I knew she wasn't going to like what I had to say about Thanksgiving, I waited until the last moment–lunch was over and we were leaving the cafeteria.

"You know the Fall Classic Tournament over Thanksgiving?" I said as we walked out into the hall. "I got invited."

The corners of Talia's mouth drooped. "You said you'd go away with us."

"No, *you* said I'd go away with you. I said I wasn't sure."

Her eyebrows dipped. "You don't want to go to Hilton Head?"

"Tal, don't do this. You know I want to go, but there'll be pro scouts at the tournament. Guys get drafted straight out of high school all the time."

Talia stopped in the middle of the hall and widened her eyes. "And not go to Rice?"

"Come on." I took her hand. My next class was on the other side of the building. Talia allowed herself to be coaxed along, and we passed a bunch of kids at a table who were asking people to sign up for some march on Washington.

"So now you're saying you're *not* going to college?" Talia repeated the question she already knew the answer to.

"I didn't say that. I said–"

"Hey, Dan," a voice interrupted us. Like a guide giving a college tour, a kid from the sign-up table started walking backward in front of Talia and me. He had long, ratty, brown hair. "How about signing up?"

6 **tournament** sporting contest – 8 **to droop** to bend or hang downward – 11 **Hilton Head** an island off the coast of South Carolina – 12 **pro** *(abb)* professional – 13 **to get drafted** to be selected – 16 **Rice** name of a university in Houston, Texas – 18 **to coax** [koʊks] to persuade

"For?" I asked.

He pointed at a poster on the wall.

> **DID YOU KNOW?**
>
> **1% OF THE POPULATION CONTROLS 25% OF ALL THE WEALTH IN AMERICA?**
>
> **THE WEALTHY OFTEN PAY FEWER TAXES THAN THE MIDDLE CLASS?**
>
> **BANKS KEEP PROFITS, WHILE TAXPAYERS PAY FOR THEIR LOSSES?**
>
> **HOMELESSNESS IN THE UNITED STATES IS AT AN ALL-TIME HIGH?**
>
> **UNEMPLOYMENT IS NEAR AN ALL-TIME HIGH?**
>
> **POLITICIANS DEPEND ON WEALTHY INDIVIDUALS AND CORPORATIONS?**
>
> **WANT TO MAKE A DIFFERENCE? JOIN THE THANKSGIVING MARCH ON WASHINGTON**

Talia pulled my hand. It was her turn to coax me away. "Dan, we were talking."

"Who do you think politicians *really* serve?" asked the ratty-haired kid. "The rich people and corporations who pay for their election campaigns, or the rest of us?"

"Dan." Talia tugged impatiently.

I let myself be pulled away.

"Think about it, *Dan*," the kid called behind me.

"Who was that?" Talia asked as we continued down the hall.

"Don't know."

"He knew your name."

"Lots of people know my name."

"He sounded like he knew you."

"They do that to get your attention."

"What do I have to do to get your attention?" she asked.

I squeezed her hand. "You *always* have my attention."

Not that she gave me much choice.

"Then please explain what's going on. First you say you're not going to Hilton Head. Now you're not going to college?" Talia loved to spin everything toward the dramatic.

"I'm going to Rice," I said patiently. "The letter of intent's supposed to come in a few weeks. The deal is basically done. But in the extremely unlikely case that I pitch lights out at the tournament, and some major-league team actually wants to sign me straight out of high school, Rice would let me go."

"And you'd really do that? Even after that coach arranged for your work study and stipend?" Talia asked. Was it any surprise that *Legally Blonde* was still one of her favorite movies? Only, unlike Elle Woods, Talia didn't start with the ditz thing and then wait until law school to discover she had brains. Talia displayed lawyer smarts whenever it suited her.

"He wouldn't be happy, but he'd understand," I tried to explain. "It's all about the big show. He knows that."

I can't say I was sorry when we reached the corner in the hall where each day we parted after lunch. As if she suddenly no longer cared about Thanksgiving or baseball, Talia smiled, all white teeth and lip gloss. "See you at eight? Carrie's party?"

Now I understood. She knew I didn't want to go to that party, but there was no way I could refuse after saying no to her family's Thanksgiving trip. Getting me to the party was probably what the whole Thanksgiving argument had been about in the first

19 **Legally Blonde** American comedy film – 20 **Elle Woods** leading actress in Legally Blonde – 20 **ditz** *(AE, sl)* silly and foolish – 22 **smarts** *(AE, pl)* know how, intelligence

place. I may have been considered an exceptional high school athlete, but once again I'd been totally outclassed by a girl who stood five feet two inches and barely weighed 100 pounds.

"We don't have to stay at the party that long," Talia assured me with a winning smile.

Defeated, I sighed. "Sure."

She stretched up and kissed me on the cheek. "Good boy."

2

In baseball the pitcher and catcher together are called the battery, which is kind of strange since when they're pitching and catching, neither is batting. It's the tightest unit on the field. Outfielders and infielders have to work together to turn plays, but no two guys have to be more in sync than the battery. Noah Williams and I had been a battery for so long that we were *beyond* in sync. We didn't only finish each other's sentences, we sometimes started them.

"Want to hit the studio? Buzzuka Joe's coming in," he said in the car after we finished working out in the school weight room that afternoon. Noah's older brother Derek had a recording studio in Burlington. While not exactly a hotbed of musical talent, the small city ten miles west of Median provided just enough homegrown bands, radio commercials, and public service announcements to keep Derek in business. Friday afternoons were reserved for local acts, and sometimes Noah and I would hang out and watch the recording sessions.

"Besides, Olivia'll be there ... *stud*," Noah kidded at a red light.

"Oh, yeah?" I yawned.

"And you act like it's no biggie." Noah smirked. "Just another fox with the hots for Handsome Dan."

I shrugged. Olivia was cute and sexy and interning at the studio. We'd flirted the last time I was there, but it was just good-natured fooling around. She knew about Talia.

The light changed and we passed a cluster of orange, blue, and military olive tents that had sprung up like mushrooms over the summer in a weedy, neglected park not far from Town Hall.

1 **pitcher** player who throws the ball at the batter – 3 **batting** act of facing the opposing pitcher and trying to hit the ball away to score points for one's team – 4 **outfielder** *Außenfeldspieler* – 5 **in synch** [sɪnk] *(inf)* working well together (*abb* for synchronized) – 5 **battery** pitcher and catcher working as a unit – 12 **Burlington** town in North Carolina – 12 **hotbed** nest – 18 **stud** *(sl)* physically attractive young man – 20 **no biggie** *(sl)* not important – 21 **fox** *(sl, AE)* sexually attractive woman – 21 **(have) the hots (for sb)** *(pl, sl)* (feel) strong feeling of sexual attraction (towards sb) – 22 **to intern** to do supervised practical training/work

It was called Dignityville and there were supposed to be homeless people living there. As we passed, a girl with curly, reddish brown hair came out of the park carrying a laundry basket. I felt a mild blip of surprise. "Is that Meg Fine?"

Noah glanced. "Yeah."

Meg had been my lab partner in chemistry the year before, and was in government and politics with me this year. I sometimes saw her at parties, although now that I thought about it, not recently.

"What's she doing there?" I wondered out loud.

"You have to ask?" Noah said.

Meg Fine was homeless?

It took about twenty minutes to get to Burlington. Derek's studio was in a run-down neighborhood of old factories, auto repair establishments, and pawn shops. Broken glass glittered along the curbs. Empty bottles inside brown paper bags littered the sidewalks.

A few blocks from the studio we passed a police car with its blue and red lights flashing. Two cops had a big tattooed man bent facedown on the hood of a dark green Range Rover. They were cuffing his hands behind his back while a young woman argued with them.

"Hey, stop," I said. "It's Olivia and Oscar."

Noah slowed down.

"Come on, pull over," I said.

"It's a bad idea, man," Noah warned.

"Just stop."

"Dan, you don't–"

"I said *stop!*"

Noah pulled to the curb and I got out in time to hear one of the cops say to Olivia: "Sorry, miss, but he's got no license or registration for this vehicle."

15 **pawn** [pa:n] **shop** *Pfandleihgeschäft*

The handcuffed man's name was Oscar, and he'd once been a promising college running back until a couple of severe concussions ended his career. Now that he was handcuffed, the cops let him straighten up.

"I told you I changed clothes and left my wallet in my other pants," Oscar tried to explain. "I work for Buzzuka Joe. This is his car."

While I watched from the sidewalk, Noah stayed in his car. We both knew why he hadn't gotten out. I leaned into the car's window. "Call the studio. See if you can get someone over here."

Noah tried his phone, listened, shook his head. "I got the message. They're probably recording."

"Then go over there and get someone."

"I hope you know what you're doing," Noah muttered, and pulled away.

The truth was, I had no idea what I was doing. I just had this strong feeling that if Oscar had been a different color, or in a different part of the city, this wouldn't be happening. By now the cops were glancing at me with puzzled expressions; this wasn't a part of Burlington where you saw a lot of white teenagers.

I cleared my throat. "Excuse me, officers, but I think there's been a mistake."

One of the cops scowled. "Sorry?" he said in a tone that implied, *And just who do you think you are?*

I took my time answering. This wasn't about changing their minds. It was about stalling while Noah went for help. Nodding at Olivia and Oscar, I said, "I'm a friend of theirs, and I'm sure everything they've told you is true."

Both cops looked at me like I was whacked. "Oh, really?" One of them snorted.

"Yes, sir. This young lady works at Williams Sound, the music studio down the street, where Buzzuka Joe is recording his new album." Buzzuka Joe was a former gangbanger turned rapper

29 **whacked** *(AE, sl)* drunk

who was a big deal around Burlington. "You gentlemen are familiar with Buzzuka Joe, right? 'If The Phone Don't Ring, You'll Know It's Me'?"

"Yeah, so?" one of the cops said.

I didn't have an answer. I'd been ad-libbing and suddenly had no libs to add.

The cops seemed to sense that I was at a loss. "Listen, kid," one of them said, "I don't know who the hell you are, but if I were you I'd disappear, pronto." He took Oscar by the arm and started to guide him toward the police car.

I stepped between them and the police car, blocking their path. The cop with Oscar stopped and gave me an astonished look, then jerked his head at his partner, who came toward me. "I'm gonna count to three before I bust you for obstruction of justice and interfering with police duties. You got that? *This is none of your business.*"

My heart was pounding and a voice in my head was screaming to get out of the way. But in my gut I knew that if Oscar were white they wouldn't have bent him over the hood of the car and handcuffed him. There was a time when I might have shrugged it off as just another of life's many injustices, but a lot of things had changed since then. I didn't budge.

"Listen, buddy, for the last time," the cop snarled. "You don't want to be a hero and you don't want to get arrested. So *move*!"

Even Oscar agreed. "He's right, man. Stay out of this."

I could feel my pulse with every breath I took. I'd never been in trouble with the police before, and this was a bad time to start. I peered hopefully down the street, but there was no sign of Noah or anyone else from the studio.

"Listen to him, Dan," urged Olivia, who'd been watching my sidewalk improv.

5 **to ad-lib** to speak without really thinking first – 6 **lib** *(here)* thoughts – 14 **to bust** *(sl)* to arrest *(verhaften)* – 22 **to budge** [bʌdʒ] to move slightly – 31 **improv** *(abb)* improvised performance

"Hey, you remembered my name," I said, grinning.

It almost seemed like she blushed. "Of course."

"Aw, for Christ's sake," the other cop growled, reaching for his handcuffs and starting toward me.

"Okay, okay." Raising my hands, I backed away. "I'm going. It's just hard to believe that you'd arrest a guy just because he forgot his wallet. Like that never happened to you?"

"You're really asking for it, kid," snapped the cop holding Oscar. He walked the big man to the police car, put his hand on Oscar's head, and began to ease him down into the backseat.

There was still no sign of Noah or anyone from the studio. In a few moments they'd take Osacar downtown and book him, or whatever it was that cops did when they arrested you. It just seemed so stupid and wrong, but I couldn't think of a way to stop it.

Oscar was in the back of the police car now, bent uncomfortably forward in the seat because his hands were cuffed behind him.

The cop started to close the door.

A horn honked. Everyone turned as Noah's car raced up and screeched to a stop. Out jumped a little guy wearing a white suit, sunglasses, and a black fedora.

Fortunately, Buzzuka Joe had a copy of the car registration, and a little while later the cops let Oscar go with a ticket for driving without a license. He thanked me emotionally. "I don't know why you did that, man, but God bless you." Shaking his large hand was like shaking a baseball mitt.

Olivia gave me a grateful hug, then added in a scolding tone, "Do you have any idea how close you came to getting popped?"

I shrugged and gave her a wink. She smiled and kissed me on the cheek. "See you at the studio."

22 **fedora** type of hat – 23 **Buzukka** [bə'zu:kə] – 27 **mitt** protective leather glove – 29 **to pop** *(AE, sl)* to be arrested by the police – 30 **wink** short movement of one eye in order to signal sth

They got into the Range Rover, leaving Noah and me on the sidewalk. Now that the danger had passed, my best friend put his hands on his hips and affected the amused patois he sometimes used in private when issues of race came up. "What de hell was *dat,* white boy? Trying to impress Olivia?"

I shook my head. "No, it just bothered me."

"Since when?"

Since everything started going against me and my family too, I thought. But what I said was, "Don't you think the guy's had enough crap in his life? His football career ends with a concussion, and now they want to arrest him because he forgot his wallet?"

"So *you* have to be the hero?"

"A man got to do what he got to do." The line from *The Grapes of Wrath,* which we'd read in school the year before, had become a little joke between Noah and me, a sort of catchall explanation anytime one of us did something that we couldn't, or didn't want to, entirely explain.

3 **patois** *(Fr)* [ˈpætwɑː] spoken form of language that differs from the standard language – 11 **concussion** damage to the brain that is caused by a knock or accident and makes you feel sick *(Gehirnerschütterung)* – 16 **catchall** *(here)* complete; covers everything

3

After watching Buzzuka Joe lay down a couple of tracks in the studio, we headed back to Median. It was dark by the time we got there. “You guys coming to Tory’s later?” Noah asked as he drove. Tory Sanchez was his girlfriend.

“We have to go to this stupid party first,” I answered glumly. “Some friend of Tal’s from dressage.”

“Why can’t she go without you?”

I gave him a weary look. “Because we’re a couple, remember?”

“Bet Olivia wouldn’t make you go to boring horse parties.”

Back at the studio I’d been Olivia’s knight in shining armor. Now that I’d “saved” Oscar, she couldn’t stop touching and flirting with me. Talk about having your ego stroked.

After that, everyone flopped on the couches and relaxed into a fun time digging on the music. It was so different from being with Talia’s dressage friends. They were all nice enough, but reserved and careful about everything they said and did. Maybe it was because they came from a world of private schools, country clubs, and fancy vacations. Of course, except for private school, that was Talia’s world too. And, to some extent, Noah’s and Tory’s, as well. But it was different when I was with them. We’d all known each other since grade school.

Noah turned onto my street. When I spotted the U-Haul van backed into my driveway, my spirits plunged faster than a two-seam fastball.

Stopping at the curb, Noah glanced at the van, but said nothing. I was pretty sure he knew what it meant, but it was something we’d never spoken about.

And we’d spoken about practically everything.

“See you later?” he asked solemnly.

6 **dressage** *Dressurreiten* – 14 **to dig on** *(sl)* to enjoy – 18 **country club** privately owned exclusive club usually with a golf course – 22 **U-Haul** American moving equipment rental company

I nodded, got out of the car, and pretended to walk up the driveway. The second Noah's taillights were out of sight, I stopped. A heavy sensation of dread had begun to mass in my chest. I'd known this day was coming sooner or later. Only I'd been clinging to the hope that it would be later.

A *lot* later.

Like, maybe, not in this lifetime.

Moving boxes were stacked in the front hall.

"That you, Dan?" Dad called from the kitchen.

"Yeah."

"Just in time for the last supper."

Welcome to my father's demented sense of humor.

I went into the kitchen, where my parents were sitting on folding chairs at a card table having bowls of homemade vegetable soup and bread. On the floor were cardboard boxes filled with kitchen utensils.

"So this is the end?" I slumped down while Mom got up and prepared a bowl of soup for me, adding boiled beef because she knew I needed extra protein in my diet. Both of my parents were vegetarians, but they were cool with me being a carnivore.

"This is the end ... buhm, buhm, buhm ... beautiful friend, the end," Dad chanted as if even now he couldn't take it seriously.

"I prefer to see it as a new beginning," Mom said.

I shook my head. "Hard to believe."

"You don't have to," Dad said. "It's just a temporary set-back, Dan. We'll get things together. You'll see."

"We've got our health," added Mom.

"Oh yeah, I forgot. Right." I pretended to agree. Like as long as we had our health it didn't matter that we were losing our home.

3 **dread** [dred] strong fear – 20 **carnivore** person (or animal) who eats meat – 25 **setback** change from better to worse

Neither of my parents had jobs. After being a stockbroker for a long time, Mom had been let go about five years ago when her firm went out of business. She'd looked for another job for almost four years before giving up. The longer you were out of work, she said, the more people believed there had to be something wrong with you, and the harder it was to find new employment.

For a while we managed to scrape by on Dad's salary as a supervisor for the Burlington Inner City Youth Sports Program. But then Dad had lost *his* job and now there was no way we could continue to live, eat, and keep up the payments on the house. The bank had started foreclosure proceedings–they were taking away our home so that they could resell it to someone else.

"When do we have to be out?" I asked, and took a sip of soup. Mom had grown most of the ingredients herself in the garden she tended in our backyard.

"Monday morning, seven a.m."

Since we'd known for months that this day was coming, my parents had sold a lot of their furniture and had put a few favorite pieces in storage, leaving only the bare essentials we needed to live. Over the weekend we would gather up that stuff and leave. Forever.

After dinner I went up to my room. I probably should have made good use of the time by packing the few things that remained–some favorite trophies, the ball I threw my only shutout with, a couple of cherished team photos, my first mitt–but I couldn't imagine being in this room without them, even for a weekend. I knew I'd wait until the last moment.

The same went for my clothes, books, and posters. I just couldn't do it now. It was too depressing. Instead, I took a shower

1 **stockbroker** person who buys and sells company shares on a stockmarket – 11 **foreclosure proceeding** *Zwangsvollstreckungsmaßnahmen* – 20 **storage** place for keeping things – 25 **shutout** *(AE)* a match (*esp* in baseball) in which you play so well that the opposing team gets no points at all

and changed. On my way out I stopped in the kitchen and called to whoever might hear: "I'm taking one of the phones."

We were down to two.

Outside Talia waited at the curb in her red BMW convertible.

"So we don't have to stay at Carrie's for more than an hour, right?" I asked as she started to drive.

"I promise I won't keep you away from Noah any longer than necessary," she half teased.

In the car's side-view mirror I watched the U-Haul van in our driveway grow smaller and then vanish in the dark. We'd moved into our house when I was two, so I couldn't remember living anywhere else. I'd thrown my first pitches to Dad in the backyard, and learned to ride a bike in the driveway. We'd had all those Christmas trees in the living room.

How soon before some other family moved in, and it would be like we'd never lived there at all?

"Please think about coming to Hilton Head with us?" Talia asked, pulling me back from those thoughts. "Didn't we have the best fun during the summer?"

"The best," I echoed dully. Talia's family had rented a house and I'd been invited to join them for a week. It had been nothing short of amazing–beautiful beaches, fun fishing, great seafood, living large–but it had been weird, too, doing all this stuff my own family couldn't come close to affording. "I appreciate the invitation, Tal, really. But I can't."

She didn't reply. While neither she nor any of my other friends knew exactly what my parents' financial situation was, you'd have to be pretty obtuse not to get a feeling that things weren't good.

We stopped at a 7-Eleven and Talia said, "Be right back," which was code for *Stay in the car while I buy stuff for the party.*

4 **convertible** *(n)* cabriolet (open-topped car) – 12 **pitch** throw of the (base-) ball – 23 **to live large** *(idm)* to live in luxury – 28 **obtuse** mentally slow

She returned with two shopping bags brimming with Diet Cokes, Mountain Dews, and an array of snacks. From there we drove to Carrie Bard's house, where I carried the bags in, as if I'd been the one who'd purchased everything.

1 **brimming with** full of – 2 **Mountain Dew** brand name of a lemonade – 2 **array** [əˈreɪ] group of things *(Auswahl)*

4

Over the weekend I wandered half-dazed through workouts, homework, helping mom pick vegetables in her garden, and–finally–packing the last of my stuff for the move. When I told Talia that we were going to stay with Mom's brother, Uncle Ron, the only question she asked was whether my parents were thinking of moving away from Median entirely. I promised her they weren't and quickly changed the subject.

I kept having this fantasy that we were losing our home only temporarily, that in a week or two something unexpected would happen and we'd get it back, or we'd get another home that was just as good.

The weird thing was, that's sort of what happened. At Uncle Ron's, Mom and Dad moved into the guest bedroom and I got the foldout couch in the downstairs activity room. Next to it was the changing room and shower for guests who used the pool and tennis court in the backyard. So that was my bathroom for now.

It felt strange:

We'd lost our home.

And moved into a much bigger, fancier one.

There must be lots of different reasons why people move in with relatives–houses burn down, parents get divorced, whatever. But I wonder if we all share one similar sensation. That of feeling adrift, like losing an anchor. Walking down the hall at school on Monday morning, I saw Meg Fine pulling books out of her locker. I stopped and stared, recalling that I'd seen her coming out of Dignityville, feeling the unexpected urge to say something, to connect with someone who, just maybe, understood what I was going through.

24 **adrift** disconnected

Unfortunately, by stopping in the middle of the hall, I'd unintentionally created a snag in the flow of bodies. Kids brushed past me, muttering as they detoured. Meg sensed something and looked up.

Our eyes met and she scowled. Suddenly I felt that I had no choice but to go over. "Hey."

"Oh, uh, hi, Dan." She swept some of that curly red hair away from her eyes.

"So, how's it going?" I asked.

Meg's forehead furrowed. "Okay," she replied uncertainly, obviously wondering why I'd asked.

She was right to wonder. It must have felt like I was coming from out of nowhere. I still had time to make up some excuse and move on, but instead, as if under remote control, I lowered my voice. "So, uh, listen, last Friday I was driving through town with Noah? And, um, I saw you."

Meg stiffened as she recalled where she'd been on Friday after school, then said, "So?" stretching the word into two wary syllables.

Moving a little closer, I softened my voice a bit more: "We just lost our house and had to move in with my uncle."

Her eyebrows dipped as if she didn't understand why I felt I had to share this with her. "I'm sorry to hear that," she said in a way that sort of indicated that she wasn't sorry, not really.

Maybe I shouldn't have been surprised by her chilly reply, but it caught me off guard. "Well, I mean, both of my parents lost their jobs. Like you and I–"

"Everyone in my family works," she cut in, a bit harshly. "Except for my dad, who's too sick to work. My mom and brother both have jobs."

At that point I should have shut up and dropped it, but I stupidly continued. "Then why are you ..."

2 **a snag** an obstruction, like a rock in a river – 2 **to brush** to touch lightly – 10 **furrowed** ['fɜːroʊ] made deep lines on her skin – 22 **dipped** moved down

"Living in Dignityville?" She finished the sentence irately. "Maybe because my father's treatments are unbelievably expensive? And my brother's got college loans he's trying to pay back? And after all that, there's nothing left?"

She was clearly upset and offended. This wasn't what I'd been hoping for. I'd thought that our common experience would give us something to talk about. But like most impulsive, poorly thought-out ideas, this one had backfired and now I felt like a jerk. "Hey, listen, I didn't mean anything bad. …"

The bell rang. We were both officially late for class. Meg rolled her eyes as if I was a complete horse's ass, and hurried away.

After school at Uncle Ron's house, Mom and Aunt Julie were in the kitchen making dinner. Dad was in the den drinking a beer and watching college football on the big flat-screen HDTV. We bumped fists. "S'up, dawg?"

I shrugged. "Not much."

"Work out today?"

"Yeah. Core stuff." I glanced at the screen. For the past two years at our house we'd had to get by on whatever the antenna on the roof would pick up for our ancient twenty-seven-inch cathode-ray TV with its dull and muted colors. In contrast the color on Uncle Ron's flat-screen was amazing, almost brighter than real.

"Who's playing?" I asked.

"Michigan Tech Huskies and Missouri Storm."

I'd never heard of either team and was pretty sure they were bottom-of-the-barrel Division III noncontenders. "Sounds exciting," I deadpanned.

"Hey, check out the drops of sweat." Dad pointed at the screen. "The individual leaves of grass." He slapped the couch. "Grab a beer."

1 **irately** [aɪˈreɪtli] very angrily – 9 **jerk** *(AE, sl)* foolish and rude person – 15 **S'up, dawg** *(AE, sl)* what's up, friend – 18 **core stuff** the most important stuff – 27 **bottom-of-the-barrel** of the lowest quality – 27 **noncontender** *opp of:* serious competitor – 28 **to deadpan** to speak in with little or no emotion (because, as here, he is not interested)

School rules forbade athletes from drinking, even during the off-season, but Dad and I had an understanding. I might have taken him up on the offer if I hadn't had homework to do.

Downstairs, my ten-year-old twin cousins, Mike and Ike (their real names were Michael and Isaac), were playing air hockey. I sat on the couch and tried to read. Adding to the racket of the puck slamming around the table were Mike's and Ike's feeble but rowdy attempts to impress me with their G-rated pre-teen trash talk.

"You're such a loser!" one of them would yell, glancing out of the corner of his eye to see if I was listening.

"You're so bad you stink!"

"I'm way better than you!"

"You wish!"

When I realized I'd read the same sentence three times and still didn't know what it meant, I knew I was never going to get anything done down there. I got up, hoping to find a quieter spot upstairs. As I passed the air hockey table, Mike paused from playing. "How long're you gonna stay here, Cousin Dan?"

"Don't know."

"Mom says you've got no place else to go," said Ike.

"For the moment."

"So you could live here forever?"

"Doubtful."

"Because you're going to college next year, right?"

"Right."

"But your parents could live here forever because all Aunt Hannah wants to do is garden and Uncle Paul's a deadbeat."

Huh? Had I heard him wrong? "Sorry?"

"Our dad said your dad's a deadbeat," said Mike.

"What is a deadbeat, anyway?" asked Ike.

3 **to take sb up on an offer** to accept the offer – 8 **rowdy** ['raʊdi] loud – 8 **G-rated** harmless, childish – 9 **trash talk** insulting language – 30 **deadbeat** lazy person

"It's when you don't have a job," Mike told his brother. "But Dad said even when Uncle Paul did have a job all he ever did was play games with poor kids in Burlington."

"Was that *really* his job?" Ike asked with kidlike wonder as if it had never occurred to him that you could get a job playing games.

"He supervised after-school sports programs so kids wouldn't join gangs," I explained.

"Dad said he could have made more money working at Starbucks," said Mike, who was leaner and meaner than his more innocent twin.

"That's not true," I said.

"Dad said so," Mike insisted, as if Uncle Ron's word was law.

I felt the impulse to argue and explain that Dad's job hadn't been about making money, but about helping disadvantaged kids have a better future. It was valuable work and probably saved some kids' lives. But I caught myself. *Why was I even having this conversation?* They were just a couple of ten-year-olds.

Upstairs, Dad waved me into the den. "You gotta see this. The Huskies are first and goal, down by four. Forty-five seconds left."

It felt a little weird, seeing my unemployed father sitting in someone else's den in the afternoon drinking a beer and watching TV. He'd had a few jobs since sports supervisor, but none had lasted. Sooner or later he'd come home saying things hadn't worked out, and he'd go back to collecting unemployment insurance.

On the TV the crowd roared. It's hard to imagine a more exciting moment in a football game. Less than a minute left to play and you're on your opponent's six-yard line with four chances to score and win. The Huskies ran three plays and got the ball to the one-yard line. It was a classic goal-line stand.

10 **leaner and meaner** *(AE, idm)* more aggressive and smart or even unkind/ evil – 20 **den** *(inf)* small room where a group (and only that group) meets informally – 26 **unemployment insurance** *Arbeitslosenversicherung*

Eleven seconds left and no time-outs. One more chance to score. The crowd was still roaring. Dad and I were on the edge of our seats.

The Huskies tried a quarterback sneak.

Bodies piled up on the goal line. One ref raised his arms as if the Huskies had scored; another ref sliced his hands as if they hadn't. The TV announcer shouted that a penalty flag had been thrown. The crowd went berserk. By now Dad and I were on our feet, totally caught up in the excitement.

That's when Uncle Ron came in. My uncle is a big, imposing man. Tall, broad-shouldered, with a barrel-size belly. When he entered a room, you knew it. He was wearing a dark suit, shirt collar open and tie pulled askew. Bags under his eyes, his hair falling onto his forehead, and his jaw so dark with five o'clock shadow you had to wonder if he'd bothered to shave that morning.

"Ron, you gotta see this," Dad said excitedly.

Uncle Ron glanced at the TV as he strode to the cabinet bar, filled a glass halfway with Johnnie Walker, knocked it back in one gulp, and poured himself another.

On the screen the refs huddled. The Huskies players had their arms up like it was a touchdown. The Storm players were chopping their hands back and forth as if it wasn't. The crowd grew quiet with anticipation. Finally the officials' huddle broke and the head ref announced that a player for the Huskies had been off side. The play didn't count. Time had run out; the game was over. The Missouri Storm had won. The crowd began to roar again and Dad clicked off the TV.

"You see that?" he exclaimed, turning to Uncle Ron. "What a finish!" My uncle's face was a blank mask. He started to take a

4 **quarterback sneak** when a player who usually plays defense runs forward with the ball to attack – 5 **ref** *(abb)* referee – 7 **penalty** foul – 8 **to go berserk** to become crazily enthusiastic – 13 **askew** [ə'skju:] not straight – 21 **to huddle** *(inf)* to get together for consultation – 22 **touchdown** scoring play worth six points – 26 **off side** *abseits*

sip of whiskey, then seemed to change his mind and knocked the whole drink back, banged the empty glass down on the counter, and stalked out of the den.

At dinner Uncle Ron's bad mood only got worse. "What is this?" he demanded when Aunt Julie placed a steaming bowl in front of him.

"Vegetable curry stew," she explained. "But we've got meat for those who want it." Mom brought over a plate piled with browned chunks of lamb and added some to his soup. "Anyone else?"

"Me, thanks," I said.

Uncle Ron glowered at the chunks of lamb bobbing in the yellowish stew, then frowned at Mom, as if he knew where Aunt Julie must have gotten the idea for this concoction. By then I'd tried the stew and a chunk of the lamb. It was pretty good, but I'd had years to get used to Mom's recipes. Ron glanced at Mike and Ike, who were chowing down on frozen individual pizzas hot from the oven. "There any more of those?"

"Seriously?" Aunt Julie asked, surprised.

"Yes ... seriously," Uncle Ron growled as if he could barely contain himself.

We ate silently while Julie put a frozen pizza in the oven, everyone keenly aware that it was time to tread on eggshells. That's when my eight-year-old cousin, Alicia, Mike and Ike's younger sister, turned to her father and said, "Daddy, what's Dignityville?"

"An incredibly stupid idea," Uncle Ron grumbled.

Alicia's eyebrows dipped. "There's a boy in sixth grade who lives there."

"Really?" Aunt Julie said. "You mean there's a homeless child at your school?"

12 **to glower** to look in an angry way – 12 **to bob** to move up and down when floating on the surface of water – 13 **stew** [stu:] *Eintopf* – 14 **concoction** mixture – 20 **to growl** to make an angry sound

"At mine, too," I said, thinking of Meg.

"You're not really homeless, Dan," Aunt Julie blurted out.

Everyone went silent.

"I … wasn't talking about me," I said.

"Oh." Pressing her fingers to her lips, Aunt Julie blushed with embarrassment. "I'm sorry."

"The boy in sixth grade?" Alicia said. "Before he moved to Dignityville he lived in a tent in the state forest. He said the school bus used to pick up a whole bunch of kids there."

"Did only children live there?" Aunt Julie asked. "What about their parents?"

As was his habit when his wife said something unintentionally inane, Uncle Ron rolled his eyes. "The parents also live there. They just don't take the school bus." He paused, his face darkening, then muttered, "Worst damn idea I've ever …"

He trailed off. No one spoke. My uncle put down his spoon. "What the hell were they thinking? Putting all those people in Osborne Park, right in the middle of town where everyone can see them. Who in their right mind would move to a town that looks like it's full of derelicts?"

It was a badly kept secret that Uncle Ron was having financial problems. He was a lawyer and had made big investments in some condominiums that now stood unfinished and empty. And just when things seemed to be getting a little better, the town council decided to erect Dignityville to house the growing number of homeless families in Median.

"I don't think the town had a choice," Mom said. As Uncle Ron's big sister, she was the only person I'd ever seen stand up to him when he got angry. "The homeless were occupying the park anyway."

"Great, so now we're giving them food, beds, and a place to go to the bathroom," Uncle Ron grumbled irately. "How long's

20 **derelict** *(n, AE)* homeless and jobless person – 23 **condominium** *(AE)* apartment which is one of many in a block

it going to be before every damn bum within five hundred miles moves here? How long before this whole town is completely overrun with them?"

"It's not meant to be a permanent residence," Mom said. "It's just a safety net for people who've fallen on hard times. Until they can get back on their feet." She reached over and put her hand on his arm. "They're not all fortunate enough to have a brother who can take them in."

Uncle Ron looked at my mother's hand. She might have had a temporary calming effect on him, but if this was anything like the past, it wouldn't last.

1 **bum** *(AE)* person without a permanent home

5

In an effort to make the downstairs rec room feel homier, I put out a few of my trophies, but it didn't work. Not only was it not my bedroom, it wasn't a bedroom, period. The space was too wide open and echo-y, and every time someone was in the kitchen or used a bathroom, the sound of water running through pipes was in my ears. Instead of a dresser with drawers, all I had for my clothes was a couple of plastic tubs, and my desk was the folding table we'd used in our kitchen before we'd moved.

With the twins and Alicia constantly going in and out to play or look for toys, it was so hard to do homework that I started going to the media center at school every chance I got. One day Meg stopped at the table where I was studying. "Hey."

"Uh … hi," I said uncertainly, the awkwardness of our last encounter still fresh in my memory.

She swept a curly reddish brown lock away from her face and bit her lip. "I think I owe you an apology."

I felt myself relax. "Oh hey, no problem. I was actually wondering if I was the one who should apologize. I mean, talk about being presumptuous."

"No more than anyone else. People hear 'homeless' and just assume drunks and vagrants. You get a little defensive." Her eyes darted away. "Well, that's all I wanted to …"

I didn't want her to go, and gestured to an empty chair. "Have a seat." She was cuter than I remembered. "You look different."

"It's what happens when you lose twenty pounds and some zits." She sat. "I call it the Homeless Diet."

"Serious?"

She smiled gently. "No. With all the fast food I've eaten I should be a hippo."

It got quiet. She glanced around. I tried to think of something to say. "So, uh, you said your dad was sick?"

13 **awkwardness** ['ɑ:kwɔrdnəs] difficulty caused by embarrassment; problematic feeling – 19 **presumptuous** rude and disrespectful – 21 **vagrant** ['veɪgrənt] person who has no home or work, a tramp – 26 **zit** *(inf)* pimple *(Pickel)*

The smile left her face. “Cancer.”

“Oh, sorry.” I wanted to smack myself. *Why did I have to bring that up? Couldn’t I have thought of something else to talk about? Too late now.* “Isn’t the government supposed to help?”

“They do, with some of it. He used to manage a restaurant and they were supposed to pay for his pension and health benefits, but they went bankrupt. There’s Medicaid, but it doesn’t cover everything.”

“If he’s that sick, shouldn’t he be in a hospital?”

Meg stared down at the table. “There’s nothing they can do. He’s just supposed to stay home and take his medicines.”

Home was Dignityville. Now I felt even worse. “Sorry, I don’t know why I brought that up.”

She glanced my way. Her eyes were hazel and pretty. “You moved in with relatives?”

“Yeah, uh, it’s just temporary.” That had become my standard line. Maybe if I repeated it enough, it would come true.

“We lived with friends for a while, but it didn’t work. It’s not easy.”

“Yeah, I’m kind of seeing that. Everyone’s stepping on each other’s toes.”

We’d stumbled into another silent patch. Meg straightened her books and glanced around. Was she thinking that she should go? I didn’t want her to. It wasn’t like I’d ever feel comfortable talking about this stuff with Talia, and even with Noah it would be awkward. “So, uh, you ever think about a part-time job?”

“I bagged groceries for a while. Me and a bunch of old people … I mean, *really* old … like in their seventies and eighties, who were doing it because they didn’t get enough social security. It was *so* depressing. I mean, the ones who couldn’t even stand up for that long? And there was this one old lady …” She trailed off, her gaze slanting away as if she was recalling something troubling.

1 **cancer** *Krebserkrankung* – 6 **health benefits** *(pl) Krankenkassenbeiträge* – 7 **Medicaid** federal and state program that helps with medical costs for poor people – 22 **patch** *here:* period of time – 29 **social security** *Rente*

"Yeah?" I coaxed.

Meg sighed. "She was always buying cat food … only someone said she didn't have a cat."

It took a second, then I got it. "Serious?"

"I don't know. It wasn't like I could ask her. The thing is, there's no reason it *couldn't* have been true. I mean, you Google people eating cat food and it turns out … like, they really do."

"It's safe?" I asked with a grimace.

"I Googled that, too. It's all cooked fish and meat. And I was thinking that as long as you had a lot of ketchup, and maybe some chopped onions? Could it be *that* much worse than what they serve in the cafeteria?"

I stared at her, feeling completely grossed out. An impish grin crossed her lips. "Had you there, didn't I?"

I chuckled and felt myself relax. "Yeah, for a second, maybe."

We smiled at each other.

"Homeless humor," I quipped. "I remember … you were kind of a wise guy last year. All that stuff you'd mutter about Ms. DiRusso in chemistry."

Meg waved her hand dismissively. "She was easy. Remember the dust explosion?"

"When her hair caught on fire?"

"And because of the safety goggles she didn't know it right away?" Meg imitated our chemistry teacher sniffing loudly. "'What's that smell?'"

We laughed and Mr. Smith, the librarian, glowered at us from the checkout counter.

I dropped my voice. "That was pretty sick."

"And when she demonstrated how to pipette acid and got a mouthful?" Meg whispered. "And she spit it out and was like, 'Guess I can skip my next cleaning at the dentist!'"

We started to laugh again.

"If you two can't control yourselves I'm going to ask you to leave," Mr. Smith said sternly.

13 **grossed out** *(AE, sl)* disgusted – 17 **to quip** to joke

"Let's get out of here." I started to gather my books.

Meg picked up hers and we left the media center. But out in the hall, there was a sort of awkward "Now what do we do?" moment. The period was almost over. But neither of us moved, as if we were each waiting for the other to say one last thing.

"So," we both said at the same time, then laughed uncomfortably.

"You first," I said.

"No, you."

"Well, uh, just glad we talked, you know?" I said. "It's not like there are a lot of people I'd … feel comfortable discussing this stuff with."

She smiled. "That's what I was thinking too."

The bell rang and kids began to pour out of classrooms. Meg gave me a little wave and disappeared into the crowd. And once again, in a school filled with friends, I felt alone.

6

One of the silver linings of life at Uncle Ron's was that his house had Wi-Fi, so I could video chat with Talia.

"Surprise!" I IM'd later that day. "W2chat?"

It took a while for her to respond. The second I saw her solemn expression on the screen, I knew something wasn't right. "So what's up?"

"Not much." Her eyes darted away, probably to the other conversations she was having.

"Hello?" I said.

Her eyes returned to me, her face blank, her lips a straight line.

"Something wrong?" I asked.

"No."

"Come on."

"Nothing's wrong." She sounded annoyed.

"Now I *know* something's wrong," I said.

Talia wasn't one to keep things in. "You can do whatever you want, Dan. I have to trust you. I mean, if we can't trust each other, what's the point?"

"Someone told you they saw me talking to Meg?"

"Not just talking, laughing."

"So I'm not allowed to laugh with another girl? Seriously, Tal, we were just riffing on Ms. DiRusso and all the dumb stuff she did last year. Don't make it into something it's not. You are my number one and onliest babe. You know that, right?"

"If you say so," she said with a sniff.

"I say so."

After that we began to chat about school and friends, but my thoughts kept going back to Meg, and how it had felt connecting

1 **silver lining** *here:* positive aspects – 3 **IM'd** *(AE, abb)* to send an instant (text) message – 23 **to riff** to talk about sth in an amusing way – 26 **sniff** when you breathe noisily in order to express your dislike

with her and speaking about things that meant something. And how a lot of what Talia and I were talking about now, didn't.

And then, seemingly from out of nowhere, a hiccup of resentment unexpectedly lodged in my throat. I didn't want to be living at Uncle Ron's, using his Wi-Fi to talk to my girlfriend. I wanted to be home, using my own Wi-Fi, in a house where the mood didn't depend on our host's daily bank balance. I wanted to go back to the life I'd had when at least one of my parents had a job, and people didn't act like my dad was a loser.

"Hey?" On the screen, Talia's expression turned softer, concerned.

"Sorry?"

"You got really quiet."

"Oh, yeah, just thinking."

I could feel the ropes that held me together beginning to tighten and fray. "But, know what? I better get off." I didn't want this knot of emotion to unravel in front of her. "Hit you back later?"

Talia frowned. "Are you sure you're okay?"

"Everything's fine, Tal. I just need to chill for a moment."

I signed off and sat there feeling like I wanted to smash something into a million pieces. I needed a window to throw a rock through, or a garden gnome to pulverize with a sledgehammer. Why did it have to be me? Of all the families in Median, *why did mine have to be homeless?*

Getting angry didn't help, but maybe a cup of tea would. It beat smoking and I had a feeling Uncle Ron wouldn't be too keen on me raiding the liquor cabinet. The hall outside the kitchen smelled of cinnamon, which meant Mom was making applesauce to sell at the farmer's market. Inside, the air was steamy and pungent. Mom was wearing a blue bandana on her

3 **hiccup** *here:* sudden feeling – 16 **to fray** to become loose – 17 **to unravel** *here:* to become apparent, be shown – 29 **cinnamon** *Zimt* – 31 **pungent** with strong smells

head and a denim shirt and jeans. For a second I flashed on the memory of when she used to get up every morning and put on black pants suits and high heels, grab her briefcase, and go.

Felt like a long time ago.

"Know where they keep the tea?" I took a mug from the shelf.

Mom pulled open a cabinet and handed me a packet of green tea.

"Kettle?" I asked.

With her finger she tapped the hot water dispenser beside the sink. I filled the mug and sat down at the kitchen counter, feeling the steam on my face while I waited for the tea to steep. Mom sieved the cooked apples, separating out the skin, seeds, and stems. "How's school?"

"Okay."

"Talia?"

"Fine."

"Your friends?"

"Okay."

"Life on Jupiter?"

"Huh?"

"Just checking. *Something's* not okay." Mom mushed cooked apples through the sieve.

We both knew why she'd said that. It had been about a thousand years since I'd sat in the kitchen and watched her cook. But I didn't want to tell her I was angry about having to live at Uncle Ron's. She would definitely think I was blaming her. Instead, I asked, "How'd you know you were going to like growing vegetables and cooking stuff?"

"I didn't."

"Then how ...?"

"I just tried it. I had to do something or I would have gone crazy. I mean, looking for jobs that didn't exist." She paused, then added, "And I was lucky. Not only did I find something I

12 **to sieve** [sɪv] to pick out

loved, but it gives me a sense of … well-being that I didn't have before."

If I hadn't seen it with my own eyes, I might not have believed it was possible to find happiness going from a high-paying corporate job to something menial like gardening that hardly paid at all.

"Is that why … it kind of seems like … what's happened to us doesn't bother you that much?" I asked.

Mom wiped her forehead with her sleeve. She had a way of looking at me, almost like she was looking *through* me, and into the place where she could see what I was really thinking. "It's really bothering *you*, isn't it?"

I almost denied it, but she'd know I was lying. So I just shrugged and nodded. "Yeah, it's like … it's always on my mind, you know? And every time I think about it, it's a total buzzkill."

A crooked, worried expression etched itself onto her face. "It's been a shock for you. Your dad and I had time to prepare for this. Maybe we tried too hard to make it like nothing in your life would change."

"But it did anyway," I said. "We stopped going on vacations and out to dinner. We got rid of cable. We had to cut back on everything."

"But your day-to-day life stayed the same." Mom picked bits of skin and seeds out of the sieve. "You still went to school and played baseball and spent time with your friends. So this … is a much bigger disruption to you than to us. I'm sorry, sweetheart. I wish it wasn't this way."

I felt some of the anger and resentment evaporate. Mom put down the sieve. She stared into the sink and then slowly brought her gaze up until her eyes met mine. "You know what I'm going to say?"

I did. About two years after she lost her job, a friend of hers convinced her to try yoga and something called mindful

15 **buzzkill** *(AE, sl)* negative event that makes you feel depressed – 16 **crooked** ['krʊkɪd] *(adj)* twisted – 21 **cable** cable tv – 26 **disruption** interruption, disorder

meditation. Mom had gone into it reluctantly, but it wasn't long before she became a full-fledged convert.

Now it was my turn to gaze down at the counter.

She slid her hand over mine. "I'm not saying it's a magic cure-all, but it helps. I don't think I could have survived the last three years without it."

Steve Carlton, one of the greatest pitchers in the history of baseball, had meditated regularly, and so had a bunch of other players. But I still couldn't see Dan Halprin doing it. "Sorry, Mom."

No surprise there, but what Mom did next was. She went to the kitchen door, peeked out, then returned. Speaking in a hushed voice, she said,"There's something else. Just between us, this isn't a good place. There's way too much negative energy."

It didn't take a rocket scientist to know who she was talking about.

"But we don't have a choice," I said.

Mom picked up an apple and began to mash it into the sieve. "There's *always* a choice."

2 **full-fledged** *(AE)* completely trained or developed – 2 **convert** ['kɑːnvɜːrt] person who has accepted a new belief

7

Call it negative energy, stress, or tension. Whatever word or phrase you chose, Uncle Ron was dealing with a lot of it. He'd leave for work at dawn, come home after dark, and still be on the phone for hours. One night at dinner, when Dad came into the kitchen singing some song about freedom being just another word for nothing left to lose, Uncle Ron's knuckles turned white around the handle of the knife in his hand, and I braced myself.

The house may have been large, but it wasn't soundproof. On another evening we waited at the kitchen table for Ron, who was on the phone in the den. Dinner was getting cold and the twins and Alicia were whining. Finally Aunt Julie went into the den to see if she could get her husband to join us. Agitated grumbling followed. We didn't hear what Aunt Julie said, and Ron surely didn't want us to hear his reply, but his harsh whisper made it back to the kitchen anyway: "No, it can't wait. Not unless you want to see us lose everything and wind up like my sister and that loser husband of hers."

I winced. Alicia's mouth fell open and the twins went silent. Dad hung his head. Mom blinked hard like she was fighting back tears. When Aunt Julie returned to the kitchen, her face was red. She said we should start dinner.

The next morning I couldn't wait to get out of that house. Was Ron right? Was Dad a loser? All my life I'd told myself that other things besides making lots of money were important, like being a good father and helping people. But now I was starting to have doubts and feel resentful. Noah's dad, Dr. Williams, was a good father, helped people, and made a good living. Why couldn't my father do that too?

7 **to brace os** to prepare os for something unpleasant or difficult – 11 **to whine** [waɪn] to make high-pitched sounds because you are unhappy or in pain – 16 **to wind** [waɪnd] **up** to end up – 18 **to wince** [wɪnts] to suddenly feel uncomfortable

It was sunny and warm, and when I went outside I heard yelling from the elementary school bus stop. A circle had formed around Mike and a bigger kid. They both had their fists up. At first it was hard to tell whether they were fooling around or serious, but when Ike kneeled behind the kid and Mike pushed him, the picture became clearer. The kid tumbled backward and my cousins pounced on him with fists flying.

Not every brawl is the same. In some, one kid just wants to prove that he's stronger and a better fighter, and once he's done that, it's over. In other fights kids really wail on each other with a fury that doesn't seem proportionate with whatever the dispute is about. You get the feeling a kid is really upset about something else altogether and just needs to find a convenient human punching bag. That definitely seemed to be the case with Mike and Ike. The irony of it struck me. Why should I be the only one in that house who felt angry and resentful and wanted to hit and break things?

Even though the kid was down, Mike kept hitting him, and Ike added a kick. You could see by the way the kid curled up into a fetal position with his arms protecting his head that he was no fighter. I knew I had to break it up. Taking my cousins firmly by the arms, I pulled them away and told them to stay put while I checked on the kid they'd been hitting. His eyes were watery, his face red and smudged with tears. I felt bad for kids like him, the gentle-giant types who other kids pick on because it makes them feel better.

"You okay?" I helped him up and brushed him off.

He nodded and wiped his nose on his arm. I guess the good thing about most ten-year-olds is they can't inflict much harm.

Meanwhile, Mike and Ike waited with arms crossed and chins jutting defiantly as if they knew what they'd done was wrong, but were still determined to claim that they were right.

8 **brawl** [brɑːl] fight – 10 **to wail on** *(sl, AE)* to hit forcefully – 20 **fetal position** bodily position with the knees up towards the chest and the head bent forward – 31 **to jut** to stick out – 31 **defiant** hostile and aggressive

"Have a seat, guys." I sat on the grass with them.

"He started it," Mike insisted.

"Doesn't matter," I said.

Mike and Ike glanced at each other uncertainly.

"You guys must be pretty angry, huh? I mean, to pound on another kid like that?"

Their foreheads bunched.

"So what are you so angry about?" I asked.

Neither answered. Mike pulled a few blades of grass out of the ground, and Ike followed his example. Maybe asking ten-year-olds to get in touch with their feelings was a bit too much. I decided to try a hunch: "How about this? Suddenly there's this other family in your house, and your father's stomping around pissed off all the time, and your mother spends half her life crying. Must be kind of upsetting, huh?"

Ike nodded without waiting to see what his brother did.

"Believe me, I know how you feel," I told them. "There are times when I want to hit someone too."

Their eyes widened with surprise and curiosity. Down the block, the elementary bus turned the corner.

"Do me a favor?" I said, getting up. "Don't beat up anybody else today. If your dad finds out it'll just make him madder. And maybe later we'll find something really cool to smash into a jillion pieces."

They nodded eagerly and got on the bus. I walked back to Uncle Ron's to wait for Noah. The truth was, I was looking forward to breaking stuff as much as they were.

That afternoon Noah and I were in the weight room at school doing oblique medicine ball tosses, down on one knee, catching, twisting, and heaving the ball back. In no time we'd worked up a sweat and were breathing hard.

7 **Their foreheads bunched** i.e. they frowned *(die Stirn runzeln)* – 14 **pissed off** *(sl, adj)* annoyed – 24 **jillion** extremely large number (this is a made-up word; there is no such number as a "zillion" in math) – 29 **oblique** [əʊ'bli:k] not straight or direct

"Think your parents have any patients who might know about part-time jobs on weekends?" I asked. "Even five, ten hours would help."

"I'll ask them." Noah caught the heavy ball and tossed it back. "Glad you feel that way."

I wasn't sure what he meant. "What way?"

"Like you want to work."

We switched positions. Now I was twisting to my left and he was twisting to his right.

"Hell, yeah," I said.

"Not like these people living in parks," Noah went on. "Half of them have college degrees. They could be working."

"Not if they can't find jobs." I wiped sweat off my forehead and thought of my parents.

"Come on," Noah scoffed. "There's all kinds of work in the energy fields up north and out west. Sometimes you just have to move. I mean, look at my grandfather. He had to move all the way from the Jim Crow South to Chicago just to be a train porter. And what about all the immigrants who come here from other countries? They're not sitting around complaining."

Noah was a solid catcher and hitter, but not a standout who could get a scholarship with a Division One school, or really think seriously about a baseball career. He loved the game and would probably play at Amherst, a Division III team, but basically he planned to follow his parents' path into medicine.

"Suppose you get out of med school and can't find a job?" I heaved the medicine ball to him.

"No way. There's always work for doctors," he said. "Maybe not in some well-to-do suburb, but in towns in the middle of nowhere ... Indian reservations ... inner-city clinics. This idea that everyone's got to get everything handed to them on a silver platter is totally whack."

15 **to scoff** to express disapproval – 18 **Jim Crow South** racist and segregated south; the persona Jim Crow was a racist character in American theatres – 21 **standout** exceptional person superior to others – 32 **whack** *(AE sl)* crazy

He heaved the ball back and I caught it. "Yeah, but aren't *you* the one who *expects* to go to med school? I mean, talk about silver platters."

"Are you serious? I worked my butt off to get into Amherst," Noah said, sweat dripping down his face. "And I'll have to do the same to get into med school. You know my father was the first one in his family to go to college? And his father was the first to eat in a desegregated restaurant? No one's handing me anything." He gestured at the ball. "Now throw it, white boy."

8 **desegregated** no longer separated by race

8

Back at Uncle Ron's the twins and I went into the garage and smashed some old toy cars and boats with hammers. It might not have been as soothing as meditation, but it was pretty satisfying until Alicia told Aunt Julie what we were doing and she made us stop.

From that day on I made a point now and then to throw a football with Mike and Ike, or play two-on-one hoops and air hockey. I'd forgotten how good it felt to horse around and play a dumb, meaningless game for half an hour, especially when the rest of the evening would be spent tiptoeing around Uncle Ron's volcanic moods.

That Friday Noah and I went back to Derek's studio to hear a new band record, and over the weekend I found some work helping one of Uncle Ron's neighbors clear brush from the back of his lot and chop some dead trees into firewood. On Sunday afternoon Talia and I went with her family to a dressage event where she placed third, and afterward we all went out to dinner to celebrate. It was fun … until they dropped me off back at Uncle Ron's and I rejoined my parents as the somewhat less-than-welcome poor relations.

One day the following week I was leaving the cafeteria with Noah and some friends from the team, talking and laughing when the ratty-haired kid at the table in the hall called out, "Hey, Dan, ready to sign up?"

I felt myself tense. All my friends, plus a couple of kids at the sign-up table, were watching and listening. "Why do you ask?"

"Seems like a good time," he said.

Had he heard that we'd lost our home? Did he think that would make me more sympathetic to his cause? "Why's that?" I gave him a hard look.

7 **two-on-one hoops** basketball practice game (*usu* one attacker and two defenders) – 8 **to horse around** to fool around – 10 **to tiptoe** to walk very carefully and quietly – 11 **volcanic** *here:* explosive

Some kids will back down when you give them that look, but this kid kept his eyes steadily on mine. "Just figured for once I had your undivided attention."

It took a second to realize that for the past few weeks I'd been with Talia every time I'd passed him, and he probably remembered that time she'd pulled me away before he had a chance to lay out his spiel. But Talia wasn't feeling well and had stayed home that day. Still, it had to take guts to stand up in front of senior athletes and call one out. I looked at the posters on the wall behind him.

400 AMERICANS HAVE MORE THAN HALF THE WEALTH IN THIS COUNTRY. **WHY IS IT EASIER TO BELIEVE THAT 150,000,000 AMERICANS ARE BEING LAZY RATHER THAN THAT 400 AMERICANS ARE BEING GREEDY?** **STOP THE WAR ON THE POOR!** **BAIL OUT SCHOOLS, NOT BANKS!**

"People are suffering," the kid said. "They can't find work, or get a decent education. You think it's fair that someone dies because he can't pay for adequate medical care while someone else with the same disease lives because he can?"

My friends started to drift away. Meanwhile, I thought of Meg's family living in Dignityville because her mom and brother had to spend practically everything they earned on medicine for Mr. Fine. I used to think that life was like sports: Things were rarely fair. The other team cheated. Your best player got hurt. You threw a perfect strike and the ump called it a ball.

But that's a game, not life.

In sports people don't die because they can't afford medicine. They don't become homeless because a company goes out of business or moves jobs overseas.

7 **to lay out his spiel** *(here)* to say what he wanted to say – 8 **it had to take guts** *(sl)* you had to be very brave and courageous – 17 **to bail out** to help – 27 **ump** *abb for:* umpire (referee) – 27 **called it a ball** *(idm)* stopped the game

I gestured at the posters. "You really think marching's gonna make a difference?"

The ratty-haired kid looked surprised. "You don't think protests changed the war in Vietnam or segregation in the South?"

I couldn't say. We may have studied those events in school, but those old protest movements were about as real to me as trigonometry. You learned what you needed to ace the test. And not for an instant did it feel like it had any actual meaning in your life.

"If we don't do something, it's only going to get worse," the kid said. "And it's not the kind of thing one person can do. Marches show strength. They tell politicians that we have the numbers and the votes to change elections."

I was more than three years away from being able to drink legally, but only months from being able to vote. Sure, voting may have been way more important, but given the choice, I would have switched those two age requirements in a heartbeat.

The kid was still waiting for me to respond.

"Can I ask you something personal?" I said. "Why do you care? You homeless or something?"

The kid gave me a long, curious look, then said, "No, I care ... because I'm *not* homeless."

***

It was one of those days when no matter how hard I tried, I couldn't get away from things I didn't want to think about. I'd signed up for government and politics because Noah said the teacher, Ms. Mitchell, graded you mostly on class participation and multiple-choice quizzes. She didn't like reading student papers, which was perfect because I didn't like writing them.

Wearing a red tent dress and big hoop earrings, Ms. Mitchell waddled in and dropped into her chair. "All right, my little gremlins, today we start our unit on local government and politics," she announced in her booming voice. "Pay attention

32 **gremlin** *here:* troublemaker

because at the end of the unit each of you will give an oral report on a topic of local interest. So what's going on around here? Do any of you ever look at the *Median Buzz*, or read that miserable excuse for a neighborhood newspaper? What are the issues?"

Ben Phillips raised his hand. "Dignityville?"

"All right, we'll start there." Ms. Mitchell gazed around. "I assume you're all familiar with it?"

Meg sat across the room and I glanced at her just in time to catch her peeking at me out of the corner of her eye. Then she seemed to go rigid and stare straight ahead. We hadn't spoken since that day a few weeks before when we'd nearly gotten thrown out of the library, and I felt a little bad about that. Of course, she didn't know about the grief Talia had given me for laughing with another girl.

"Okay, for those of you who've been hiding under rocks, Mayor George and the town council decided a while back to create a tent city in Osborne Park to house the homeless," Ms. Mitchell explained. "If you've been in town you can't miss it. Does anyone know why they decided to do that?"

Susan Barrow raised her hand. "To save money."

"How would a tent city save money?" Ms. Mitchell asked.

"Because they'd all be in one place?" Susan guessed.

"Right," said Ms. Mitchell. "Just because people are homeless doesn't mean they don't deserve the same services as the rest of us, whether that's sanitation, or medical care, or public transportation. And given the financial problems towns and cities are facing these days, I don't think anyone can blame the mayor for trying this. Here's my next question: What do *you* think of Dignityville? Is it right to round up all the homeless and put them in one place?"

Ms. Mitchell was big on critical thinking. And sometimes on just trying to get us to think, period. Since class participation

3 **miserable excuse for a ...** *(idm)* terrible, useless – 9 **to peek** to look quickly – 13 **to give sb grief about sth** to tell sb off about sth, give them a bad time for doing sth – 25 **sanitation** providing clean water and toilet facilities

was a big part of our grade, you could usually count on the GPA zombies like Ben Phillips and Susan Barrow to speak up. Now Ben raised his hand. "They can't really *force* them to move there, can they?"

"No," said Ms. Mitchell. "All the town can do is point out the benefits, like free meals, electricity, and washing facilities. But there's another reason why the idea appears to be working. Does anyone know what it is?"

Susan raised her hand. "The homeless feel that banding together makes them more visible and harder to ignore."

"Very good," said Ms. Mitchell. "When they were scattered around town, they were easier to miss. Most of you probably didn't know that there were half a dozen families living in the state forest out on High Bridge Road. Hardly anyone knew they were there. There were families living in cars and boats. I don't think anyone realized how many there were. And why don't they want to be ignored?"

Ben's hand went up again.

"Let's see if we can get someone else involved." Ms. Mitchell scanned the room.

It was time to gaze out the window.

"Dan?"

An invisible weight pushed down on my shoulders. Do teachers get special training for picking the student who least wants to be called on?

"Why don't the homeless want to be ignored, Dan?"

Kids turned to look at me. I even heard a few chair legs scrape. I thought about the ratty-haired kid and his crusade in the hall outside the cafeteria. "Because then nothing will ever change."

Justin Smith's hand went up, which was kind of interesting because he was a gearhead auto-tech troll, not a GPA zombie.

1 **GPA** *(abb)* grade point average *(Durchschnittsnote)* – 28 **crusade** campaign – 31 **gearhead** *(sl)* person who is enthusiastic about technical devices – 31 **troll** unpleasant and ugly creature

"If they want things to change they should get off their butts and find jobs."

That was the same thing Noah had said. And yet, you couldn't find two more different kids.

Beth Perkins, an emo-punk type with dyed red streaks, turned to him. "Sure, Justin, they could work at McDonald's. But suppose you went to college and maybe even got a master's degree in business or engineering? Would you be happy flipping burgers?"

Justin tucked his chin down. "If that was the only job I could get."

"And what if you had a family?" Beth asked. "And there was no way you could earn enough at McDonald's to house and feed them?"

Justin shrugged. "I'd make sure they got a lot of Happy Meals."

The class laughed. I glanced again at Meg and saw that she was smiling. Given that she and her family were homeless, it seemed kind of remarkable.

When the period ended, I made sure we left the room at the same time. Her eyes darted uncertainly at me when we started down the hall together.

"How's it going?" I asked.

"Why do you ask?" she replied stiffly, not looking in my direction.

"Just because of what we were talking about in class."

"You're wondering why I didn't say anything?" Her voice was ripe with defensiveness. "Like why I didn't raise my hand and claim to be an authority on Dignityville?"

"No."

"Then what? Why are you even talking to me? Why are we walking together?"

I thought I understood her guarded attitude. Sometimes something happens with someone, and you don't think much about it. But what you don't realize is that the other person has

5 **emo-punk** genre of hardcore punk music – 5 **dyed** colored – 5 **streak** *Strähnchen*

thought *a lot* about it. Maybe they've even gotten kind of worked up over it. I'm not saying that day in the library when we laughed meant more to her than it did to me. It did mean something to me. But maybe it just meant something different.

We passed an empty classroom. "Come in here for a second?"

Meg frowned. "Why?"

"Just do it."

We went in. Meg crossed her arms, her eyebrows dipping. "What? You can't be seen with me in the hallway? I'm a pariah now?"

I did the two-finger swipe. "Two points for vocabulary."

She wasn't amused. "So?"

"You're not a pariah. I just have a girlfriend with spies everywhere."

She blinked, as if astonished. "*That's* why you've been ignoring me?"

So I was right. She thought I'd been ignoring her. No wonder she sounded hurt and defensive. Look at it from her point of view: I'd started to get friendly, we'd really connected, and then I'd backed away. "Sorry, I didn't mean to make it seem that way. I ... there's actually been a bunch of times when I wanted to talk to you."

"But you were afraid *she'd* find out?" Meg rolled her eyes. "Boy, Mr. Popular Stud, I'm glad I'm not in your shoes."

Ouch! This girl didn't pull any punches.

She quickly looked around the room. "Wait! What if she's got all the classrooms bugged?"

"Very funny. No, I just ... I don't know. Tal and I are pretty happy together."

"Oh, yeah, that's *so* obvious," Meg replied facetiously. "My best relationships have *always* been with people I was afraid were spying on me."

1 **worked up** *adj* very upset – 9 **pariah** [pəˈraɪə] social outcast – 11 **swipe** fast movement – 20 **to back away** to stop being involved – 24 **stud** *(sl)* attractive young man – 30 **facetious** [fəˈsiːʃəs] humorous

That made me chuckle. "You're pretty sarcastic."

"Yeah, well, I can't blow myself up like a puffer fish and show my spines when attacked."

"You're under attack?" I asked, confused.

"From embarrassment and humiliation? Duh. You *especially* should know that."

Now I got it. "Hence the pariah comment?"

"Welcome to my world," she muttered, skidding across the ice from sarcastic to bitter. She raised her head as if she'd just thought of something. "By the way, are we still keeping that secret about why you're living at your uncle's house?"

Before I could answer, the classroom door opened. Maybe I swiveled around a little too quickly to see who it was–a kid I didn't know. "Sorry, wrong room." He backed out. When I turned back to Meg, she had a thoughtful expression. "So which is it? Afraid of being caught consorting with the homeless? Or just of her jealous wrath?"

"Neither."

But she'd already turned toward the door. "Gotta get to my next class. You better stay here and count to ten so no one sees us leave together."

She went out.

I stood there *way* past a ten count, wondering … how right was she?

1 **to chuckle** to laugh softly – 16 **to consort with** to spend time with – 17 **wrath** [ræθ] fierce anger

9

“You *sure* that’s what you want to wear?” Noah asked. It was Friday night and I’d just gotten into his car. He was wearing sweatpants and an old hoodie.

“Aren’t we doing some church thing?” I said.

“We’re *cooking*. For Dignityville.”

“Be right back.” I jogged back into Uncle Ron’s, quickly changed clothes.

“You okay?” Noah asked when I returned.

“I think so, why?”

“I don’t know. You seem a little out of it lately.” He started to drive.

“Everything’s cool.” It wasn’t. And now here was the idea of cooking for the homeless, which felt strange considering my family’s current situation. There’d been a time when it would have been just another excuse to hang out with friends, no different from really, making a fire at the beach or going to the movies. But now?

Saint Stephen’s was the biggest church in town. When Noah and I got downstairs, Tory and Talia and a couple of others had already gathered around the big countertop island.

“Glad you two could make it,” Tory said in a snarky tone.

Noah clapped me on the shoulder. “Wonder Boy here was dressed for dinner with the archbishop.”

I sidled up to Talia, who gave me a concerned look and a quick peck on the cheek.

“Did you say we were cooking for Dignityville?” I whispered.

“Yes.”

That was weird, because I couldn’t remember her telling me. Was Noah right about me being out of it?

Tory tapped a metal ladle against the countertop, upon which were bags of beans, onions, and other ingredients. She was a

10 **out of it** confused, disoriented – 21 **snarky** rudely sarcastic – 24 **to sidle** ['saɪdᵊl] **up** to walk towards sb slowly and shyly – 30 **ladle** ['leɪdᵊl] long spoon used for serving liquids

planner and organizer (did someone say "control freak"?). If twenty years from now she became governor, I wouldn't be surprised.

"Order in the court," she said. "Dignityville doesn't have a kitchen, so dinners are prepared by volunteers off-site. Tonight that's us, so let's have fun while doing something good, okay?"

Everyone got to work. Noah and I were assigned to the onions.

"Punishment for being late," he muttered while Tory's back was turned.

"Why?" I whispered.

"You ever chop onions?"

I shook my head. Cooking wasn't my thing, and besides, Mom was so good at it. Noah smirked and handed me an industrial-size knife.

In no time we both had tears running down our cheeks.

"Aw, look at duh big stwong ath-a-weetes cwying," Ben Phillips teased in his best Elmer Fudd imitation. He might have been a GPA zombie in government and politics class and president of our school's chapter of Young Entrepreneurs, but what he had in brains he lacked in brawn, and seemed to have a chip on his shoulder about being on the chubby side and unathletic.

"It takes a strong man to cry." Noah wiped his eyes on his sleeve. "Something you wouldn't know about, Ben."

"Enough," Tory quickly interjected. "We're in a house of brotherly love, remember?"

The stoves were on, everyone was busy, and it started to get hot. Noah and I peeled off our hoodies. The girls were chattering, and the guys, now stirring big pots of chili, looked like they just wanted to finish quickly and go hang out at someone's house. I guess I shouldn't have been surprised when I felt something bounce off my shoulder. Turning, I found a clove of garlic lying

5 **off-site** in a different place – 16 **duh big stwong ath-a-weetes cwying** "two big strong athletes crying" – 17 **Elmer Fudd** fictional cartoon character – 20 **brawn** muscular strength – 20 **to have a chip on one's shoulder** *(idm)* to be aggressively over-sensitive about sth – 31 **clove of garlic** *Knoblauchzehe*

on the floor and saw Zach Raines, a switch-hitting outfielder who doubled as a relief pitcher, give me a furtive glance. He couldn't really be proposing a food fight, could he?

I continued to stir. A moment later a clove must have hit Noah, because he swiveled around.

"Ignore it," I whispered.

"Hell, no," Noah whispered back. He picked up the clove, waited until the coast was clear, and threw it.

In no time another clove bounced off the pot of chili and another made a little *clink* when it struck the stove hood above us. Then one landed *in* the chili. I started to get an uncomfortable feeling that had nothing to do with whether Tory caught us. This was food people were going to eat.

Noah glanced in Tory's direction to make sure she wasn't looking, then rifled the cap from a bottle of chili powder at Zach. It missed and made a loud enough *clack!* for Tory to turn and look. Instantly, the guys all pretended to focus on cooking, but the second Tory turned away Noah and I were pelted by half a dozen cloves. As Noah searched for something to throw back, Ben cleared his throat loudly: "Hey, Tory, you want to come over here and make sure I'm browning the beef right?"

It was a warning for us to stop fooling around. Obviously Ben was also feeling uncomfortable. But unlike us "big stwong ath-a-weetes," he'd had the courage to do something about it.

When the chili was done, we poured it into big plastic containers and put it in refrigerators, where it would be stored until it was reheated and taken over to Dignityville. Then Tory invited everyone back to her house for a little "reward celebration" for doing good work. Her father owned Pizza Grandé, a chain of pizza places with a Hispanic theme, and they must have been doing really well, because the Sanchezes had this amazing rec

1 **switch-hitter outfielder** in baseball *beidhändig schlagender Außenfeldspieler* – 2 **relief pitcher** *Ersatzwerfer* – 15 **to rifle** ['raɪfəl] to throw with high speed – 18 **were pelted** were attacked and hit frequently – 31 **rec** *(abb)* recreation **rec room** place where you hang out

room downstairs with a pool table, bigscreen TV, and some cool old arcade video games like Space Invaders and Pac-Man. At least one night every weekend we wound up hanging out there with Tory's parents providing pizzas and only half joking that they liked having us around because that way they knew where Tory was.

Talia and I sat on the couch with Tory and Noah while some of the others shot pool or played arcade games. While Tory and Talia talked about going to the mall the next day, I couldn't help thinking that a few miles away my bed was a couch in a rec room not so different from this. Suddenly it felt strange being with these kids who all had their own homes, while I wondered if, the next time I needed clothes, I'd be forced to go to Goodwill instead of the mall.

Talia turned to me. "You're quiet tonight."

I shrugged. "Just thinking."

No one said a word.

"What? Is that so strange?" I asked.

"Definitely." Noah grinned.

Tory's mom came to the door to announce that the pizzas had arrived. There was a mass exodus toward the stairs, but I noticed that Ben was in the middle of a Space Invaders game. "Be up in a second," I told Talia, then waited.

Ben kept playing, but I knew he'd seen me out of the corner of his eye. I didn't know him that well. Talia had told me that once a month the Young Entrepreneurs invited a local businessperson to speak, and they'd asked her father, who told her afterward that he'd been seriously impressed with how Ben had grilled him about his real estate business.

Ben finished the game, turned to me, and frowned as if to say, *Why aren't you upstairs chowing down?*

"Nice move before," I said, and as his eyebrows dipped toward puzzlement, I added, "in the church kitchen."

2 **arcade game** a machine for entertainment in a large public room – 13 **Goodwill** non-profit store that sells clothing and goods that have been given to them at very low prices – 31 **to chow down** *(inf)* to eat heartily

Ben nodded slowly, his eyes never leaving mine."Thanks ... It's too bad, you know?" He went past me and up the stairs. I stayed behind for a few moments, wondering what he'd meant. Was it too bad about the people who had to live in Dignityville? Or too bad about what had happened to me? Or was it that in his eyes, there was no difference?

10

Noah and I usually went for a long run on Saturday mornings to keep the cardio thing going. When I got back to the house after the run, Dad was in the driveway, putting Uncle Ron's Callaways in the back of our car. "Got time for a round?" he asked.

Maybe once a year Dad and I played golf at the public course just to spend time together. I knew it was a Saturday, and not a great day for him to look for a job, but given our circumstances, it still didn't feel right. Besides, once again I had a chance to earn some money helping Uncle Ron's neighbor do yard work.

"Don't think I can, sorry."

"You sure?"

I almost asked if *he* was sure going golfing was the right thing to do. I was going to spend the afternoon working; why wasn't he?

***

I worked for about four hours, and had gone back to Ron's to take a break, when Mike and Ike burst into the rec room.

"Your dad's in trouble!" Mike announced excitedly.

I went upstairs. Dad and Ron, both wearing golf clothes, were standing in the front hall. Ron's face was red and I got the feeling that he'd been chewing Dad out big-time. They both gave me a look that said I should make myself scarce.

In the kitchen Mom and Aunt Julie, dabbing her eyes with a tissue, were at the counter. Mom looked grim, although it seemed a little strange that Aunt Julie was the one who appeared really upset.

"What happened?" I whispered.

"Ron came home to play golf and your father had taken his clubs," Mom replied.

The implication hit me. "He took them without asking?"

4 **Callaway** brand name for golf clubs – 22 **to chew sb out** *(inf)* to angrily criticize sb – 22 **big-time** very much – 24 **to dab** to touch lightly and quickly

"Ron's been in the office every Saturday," Aunt Julie explained. "There was no reason to think he'd take off early today."

It seemed odd that she was defending Dad, but I had a feeling it was because Mom felt the way I did–that there was no excuse for taking those clubs without asking. But that was the kind of thing Dad sometimes did. More thoughtless than malicious, but bad judgment just the same.

Aunt Julie left the kitchen to find Alicia and get her out of earshot in case there was a round two between Ron and Dad.

"This isn't working," Mom said in a low voice now that we were alone. "The negative energy in this house is overwhelming."

"You can't blame Ron for being angry," I said. "I mean, what Dad did was incredibly dumb."

"I know, but it's still unbearable here. He's *always* angry. I feel like I can't breathe."

"What can you do?"

Mom tapped a finger against the kitchen counter and gazed off. "We'll see."

When you're a kid, things are mostly black and white, good and bad. Then you get to be a teenager and you start to see the gradual hues in between. Is someone good or bad? Both? A little more of one than the other? Dad stayed home with me when I was little because as a stockbroker Mom was making more money than he was and they didn't want to put me in day care or have some other person raise me. Think being a stay-at-home dad is easy? Even as a little kid I was aware of the looks other moms gave him in the supermarket, and at school when he volunteered for the book fair. And it's not so hard to imagine what it must have been like for him at parties with the other fathers talking about their jobs as lawyers and bankers and whatever.

6 **malicious** very unkind – 14 **unbearable** intolerable – 21 **hue** [hju:] color

But he took all that crap for my sake, and guided me toward pitching, which is probably the best thing that I ever did.

On the downside? He didn't have the best judgment. Not a lot of ambition, either. Liked to play more than he liked to work. Took his brother-in-law's golf clubs without asking.

***

"Think of it this way," Dad said in the car later that afternoon. "It's not that much different from any other campground."

I didn't know what to say. We were parked on the street across from Dignityville. Earlier that afternoon Mom and Dad went somewhere while I'd gone back to Uncle Ron's neighbor's to work. It hadn't occurred to me to ask where they'd gone.

Now I knew.

It was getting close to sunset, and inside Dignityville people were filing into the big tent in the middle of the park. A few were the grungy types you imagined homeless people to be–old guys with greasy hair and scraggly beards, ladies wearing too many sweaters. But others looked as neatly dressed as anyone who had a home.

The weird thing was, sitting there in the car, it felt like a scene out of *The Grapes of Wrath*–the Joads pulling up to a Hooverville. All I could think was, *They can't really want me to live there, can they?*

"Just have a look, Dan." Dad reached for the door handle. Mom gazed over the seat at me with obvious concern. "Try to keep an open mind."

"There's no place else we can go?" I asked.

"Not if we don't want to feel beholden to whomever we're staying with," Mom replied.

I couldn't believe they were serious. So what if Uncle Ron's house was filled with negative energy? It had to be a hundred times better than living in a tent.

16 **grungy** ['grʌndʒi] dirty, filthy – 17 **scraggly** untidy, unkempt – 21 **Hooverville** settlement of temporary housing made of cardboard boxes, plastic sheets etc. Named after the then (1929) US President Herbert Hoover during the Great Depression – 28 **beholden** grateful by necessity

We crossed the street and went through the entrance. A big handwritten sign said:

WELCOME TO DIGNITYVILLE
We Thrive on Mutual Respect and Tolerance
No violence is tolerated.
No weapons are allowed.
Sobriety is required.
No verbal or physical abuse will be tolerated.
Anyone who cannot respect these rules will be asked to leave.
If they do not leave voluntarily, the police will be called to remove them.

"Is Aubrey around?" Dad asked a heavyset guy with shaggy eyebrows and a thick bushy beard.

"He went over to the church to get dinner," the guy answered, then pointed. "There he is."

A dented old van had pulled up to the entrance and a couple of people started off-loading big pots.

"Hey, Aubrey!" The heavyset guy waved and gestured at my parents and me. A tall, thin fellow with a neatly trimmed beard started toward us. Here in Dignityville beards and plaid shirts were definitely the go-to look.

"So, you must be Dan." Aubrey offered his hand. It was obvious my parents had told him they'd be bringing me over for a visit. "Come on, let's take the tour."

I noticed right away that there was something earnest and welcoming about Aubrey, but it didn't matter. This was seriously out of the question. Dignityville was basically a refugee camp: bottom of the barrel, end of the road. Maybe other people belonged here, but not my family. And not me.

4 **to thrive on** to do well with – 7 **sobriety** [sə'braiəti] *opp of* drunkenness

As if Aubrey sensed what I was feeling, he tried to lighten the mood by making jokes. The dining tent was the "Grand Ballroom," empty campsites were "deluxe building lots," and the washing facilities and row of tall blue portapotties were the "International Spa."

"And here are the meadows." Aubrey led us around the portapotties to a plot of bare ground, weeds, and brush. "When I gave your parents the tour this afternoon, your mom thought this would be a good place for a garden, which would be a huge step toward making Dignityville self-sustaining." He put his hand on my shoulder and led us back. "There's a company that might donate some used solar cells. They're not as efficient as newer models, but they'd do. We might even go with a small wind turbine. Imagine Dignityvilles all over the country, Dan. Self-contained, self-sustainable eco-villages where people who've lost their homes will feel welcome and good about themselves. Like pioneers in the new world."

"I thought Dignityville was supposed to be temporary," I said.

Aubrey gave me an appraising look. "You follow the news, Dan?"

"A little."

"So maybe you've heard that conditions around the country are getting a little better? But unemployment's still high. People are still losing their homes. Towns and cities are having a really tough time. Believe me, Dan, nothing would make me happier than seeing everyone get a job and be able to afford a place to live, but in the meantime shouldn't we be preparing for the possibility that it might *not* happen? You can think of Dignityville as temporary if you want, but I wouldn't be surprised if twenty years from now it's still here."

I understood that he was trying to spin it in a positive way. Maybe *he* believed what he was saying, but I didn't. To me

4 **portapotty** brand name for a movable toilet – 14 **self-contained** not dependent on others – 15 **self-sustainable** self-sufficient – 19 **appraising** critical – 31 **to spin** *(inf)* to tell

Dignityville wasn't the future. It was a bunch of tents and portapotties for unlucky people who'd otherwise be sleeping in doorways and old cars. My family may have fallen on hard times, but we weren't like these other folks. I couldn't say it to Aubrey, but we just didn't belong here.

By now the Grand Ballroom was crowded with people eating on plastic plates. A humming generator in the background provided electricity for the lights. The air smelled of diesel exhaust.

"Hungry?" Aubrey asked.

It was dinnertime and I should have been, had my stomach not been knotted anxiously at the prospect of moving here.

"Come on, take a look." Aubrey pulled back the clear plastic sheets that formed the walls of the dining tent. "Any different from lunchtime in the cafeteria?"

It was, but maybe not as much as I might have imagined.

"Let's give it a try," Dad said.

I didn't want to, but couldn't figure out how to say so without sounding like a brat. We got in line. It was strangely quiet inside the tent. A few low conversations took place here and there, but mostly people were focused on eating. On the other side of the serving table a couple of volunteers in white serving aprons were ladling out ... chili.

I hardly ate, not because I knew what had gone into making that chili, but because I had zero appetite. I kept telling myself this couldn't be happening. My parents couldn't really be serious about moving to Dignityville. We weren't these people. *We* were supposed to be the ones volunteering to help *them*.

By the time we got into the car to go back to Uncle Ron's, I'd begun to prepare my arguments. But Mom had prepared hers as well: "I know you don't want to do this, sweetheart, but I feel

19 **brat** *(inf)* impolite child – 23 **to ladle** to serve with a long-handed spoon

very strongly about it. It won't be easy, but I truly believe it's the best thing we can do as a family. There's a positive energy there, and we can be part of it."

I said exactly what was on my mind. "If we go there, everyone's going to think we're homeless."

In the front seat, Dad and Mom glanced at each other. Then Mom looked back at me. "We won't be homeless. Dignityville will be our new home. We'll be on the forefront of a new way of living. You heard what he said. Someday, there'll be lots of Dignityvilles."

"I get that, Mom, but that's far in the future. Right now the people in Dignityville aren't on the forefront of anything, except homelessness."

The wrinkles around Mom's eyes deepened. "Are you worried about what your friends are going to think?"

It wasn't just my friends; it was everyone. We may have been having a tough time financially, but as long as we were at Uncle Ron's, at least we had a home. "We just don't belong there, Mom."

"That's a mindset, sweetheart. You need to think positively about this."

Positive thought ... yoga ... meditation ... those were her things, not mine. "Okay, you want to know the truth? Yes, I am worried about what my friends are going to think. I'm worried what *everyone's* going to think. Because basically, they're all going to think we're losers."

"If they're real friends, it shouldn't matter," Mom said.

Just then Dad caught my eye in the rearview mirror. The look he gave me told me to stop arguing and go along with it.

"Have we ever done wrong by you?" Mom asked.

I sat back and didn't answer. It was hard to remember the last time I'd felt this miserable. For most of my life–at least until I was twelve or thirteen–my parents had made the important

8 **to be on the forefront** to be in a leading position of a new development – 19 **mindset** ['maɪndset] general attitude

decisions for me. Since then we'd shared decisions, or I'd made them on my own. But looking back, I couldn't remember them ever deciding something for me that was so totally, absolutely misguided.

11

The next morning I got up early to clear brush and chop wood with Ron's neighbor again. While in the bathroom I glanced outside and saw Mom and her brother strolling across the backyard toward the tennis court. I had a feeling they'd gone outside because Mom didn't want the rest of us to overhear what would be said.

As I watched, I tried once again to make sense of what Mom was thinking. How was it possible that a home as beautiful as this, with its own swimming pool and tennis court, was filled with negative energy, while a tent camp of homeless people was filled with the positive stuff? And yet, if I was really honest with myself, I'd felt it too. Maybe because that Aubrey guy was so full of enthusiasm and hope, two emotions that were severely lacking in Uncle Ron's household.

But I still couldn't see myself living in Dignityville. Living in a rec room sucked, but it was way better than a tent.

While I couldn't hear the conversation Mom and her brother were having, my uncle's body language made it look as if he was arguing *against* Mom's plan. Had I been asked to predict, I would have thought he'd pretend not to like it, but secretly be pleased to get rid of us (or at least rid of Dad). But Ron's hands were on his hips and he kept shaking his head as if he absolutely wouldn't hear of it.

Go Ron! I thought hopefully.

Finally, Mom put her hand on his shoulder and said something that ended it. Ron hung his head, and Mom hugged him. I could almost hear what she was saying. Something like: I appreciate you wanting us to stay, and no matter what happens, you're my brother and I'll always love you.

Damn ...

16 **to suck** *(inf)* to be very bad – 19 **to predict** to foretell

Later that afternoon we once again parked on the street across from Dignityville. Only this time the car was packed with clothes, camping gear, and supplies. The only difference between us and the Joads was that they'd had a beat-up old Hudson truck and we had a beat-up old Subaru.

Mom looked over the seat at me. "Ready?"

"No."

In the front seat Mom and Dad shared a quick glance.

"We don't have to do this today," Dad said. "We probably have enough money to spend a few nights in a motel. The problem is, once we run through that we'll still wind up here, only with nothing in our pockets."

Mom looked over the seat at me again. "I know this is difficult, sweetheart. I know it's not what you want. But I want you to give it a chance. I promise, if you still hate it after a week or two, we'll try to come up with something else."

"Seriously, Mom? Then why bother? I know I'm going to hate it."

"Maybe not. I'm just asking you to try."

I wanted to argue, but there was no point in it. Mom was going to have her way.

Our new address was site number thirty-seven, a square plywood platform raised about six inches off the ground. Aubrey wasn't around, so we were assisted by Wade, rail thin and scruffy with a red bandana around his forehead and long graying hair in a ponytail.

"We don't have a lot of rules," he said as he helped us raise the tent and secure it to the plywood platform. "You probably saw the board when you came in. The only thing I'd add is no loud music or talking after nine o'clock. A lot of folks have to get up early for work. Aubrey told you about the hot dinner every

4 **Joads** fictional family in *The Grapes of Wrath* which loses their farm during the Great Depression and migrate to California where they hope to find work – 4 **beat-up** damaged, old – 23 **plywood** several layers of wood that are stuck together – 24 **rail thin** extremely thin *(spindeldürr)* – 24 **scruffy** shabby, untidy

night, right? As far as other meals, you'll have to fend for yourselves."

"What do people do?" Dad asked.

"The regular things. Some prepare their own on camp stoves. Some go to Subway or the diner. The hard-luck cases'll eat at the church or the food pantry. And if you do prepare food here? Don't forget to separate out your recyclables just like you did at home. Oh, and you get these."

He handed out three small booklets of bus passes. "Two free trips a day for work or appointments. And don't forget to sign up for kitchen detail. Everyone volunteers at least once a week to either serve or clean up. Of course, you're welcome to do it more often if you feel like it."

Wade left. To be honest, I felt paralyzed by the numbness of disbelief. My parents had both gone to college, and I was on my way next year. We'd had a house. They'd had jobs. This wasn't supposed to happen to people like us.

Mom and Dad rolled out their sleeping pads and bags. Having done a lot of camping in the past, we had our own gear, but we hadn't used the tent in years and it smelled unpleasantly musty. My parents shot quick looks at me. I still hadn't moved.

Dad said, "There's no rush, Dan." Which basically meant, *There's no point in standing around.*

Despite the smell the tent was pretty spacious and had room for plastic shelving for our clothes, and stackable plastic bins for our personal stuff.

"I wouldn't leave anything valuable lying around," Dad said, glancing at Mom to see if she agreed.

She nodded.

"Like my laptop?" I asked.

"Can't hurt to keep it out of sight," she said.

1 **to fend for os** to look after os – 5 **diner** *(AE)* small restaurant that serves cheap meals – 6 **food pantry** location where free food is given to people in need – 7 **recyclables** *(pl)* things that can be used again – 20 **musty** unpleasant due to a lack of fresh air

"Under your dirty underwear," Dad suggested with a wink.

That reminded me: "Where do we wash clothes?"

"There's a Laundromat about a block away," Mom said.

Right. I'd seen Meg with that laundry basket. Looked like I'd be joining her. I reached for my sleeping bag and unrolled it. This move was real. It was happening. And there was nothing I could do about it.

For now.

"So," Mom said once we'd settled in, "shall we go for a walk?"

Dad and I shared an uncomfortable look. All along I'd sensed that while he was trying to be supportive of Mom, he wasn't completely stoked about Dignityville either.

"Remember what Aubrey said," Mom reminded us. "Don't look at this as a place for the lost and disenfranchised. Imagine a day when there are hundreds of Dignityvilles, and all kinds of people live in them not because they *have* to but because they *want* to."

I felt myself wince inside. It sounded like Mom had taken a big gulp of Aubrey-flavored Kool-Aid. Dad put his arm around her. "You're right."

They both turned to me. "Coming?"

"I have to do some reading for school," I said.

"It's a little dark in here," Mom said. "Why don't you go over to the dining tent?"

"This is fine," I said, thinking, *No way am I going over there.*

Dad turned on the LED lantern. The tent filled with light. "That better?"

"Thanks."

"See you in a bit," Mom said with forced cheerfulness as if telling me to feel better.

3 **Laundromat** brand name for a location which has coin-operated washing machines – 12 **stoked** *(sl)* excited – 14 **disenfranchised** [ˌdɪsɪnˈfræntʃaɪzd] not feeling part of society – 18 **to wince** to suddenly feel very uncomfortable

They left. Feeling completely bummed, I sat down in one of the camping chairs. The tent may have been big, but it was still way smaller than my old bedroom. The low, slanting ceiling made me feel claustrophobic, and I kept getting distracted by the conversations of people as they passed outside.

Mom had promised that if, after a week or two, I still really hated it, we'd try something different.

I couldn't wait.

1 **bummed** *(sl)* miserable, worthless – 3 **slanting** *schräg, abfallend*

12

At dinnertime I convinced my parents to let me treat them to Subway with the money I'd made working with Uncle Ron's neighbor. They knew exactly why I was doing it, and I guess they went along because they sensed I could take only so much of Dignityville on our first day.

It was dark when my alarm went off the next morning. I woke with the kind of confused jolt you feel when you think you've only just fallen asleep. But there was no confusion about where I was. I'd spent too much of the previous night lying awake, staring at the ceiling of the tent, to have any doubts. It was Monday morning, and today, for the first time, I would make my way to school … from Dignityville.

Sleeping pads are okay for camping, but they're not mattresses, and I felt stiff. I'd laid out my clothes so that I wouldn't have to turn on a light when I got dressed. I knew the alarm would wake my parents, but I was hoping they'd just go back to sleep.

I was half-right.

"Where are you going?" Mom whispered from her sleeping bag.

"School," I whispered as I sat up with my back to her and pulled my pants on.

"This early? What about breakfast?"

"I'll pick up something on the way."

"And a shower?"

"At school."

I waited for her to say more, but she didn't. Pulling on a jacket, I went outside. The air was dark and chilly, but I wasn't the only one up. Light peeked out of other tents, and a few people were already out and about. A guy wearing a robe and flip-flops carried a towel and a toilet kit toward the showers. A dog trotted past.

1 **treat sb to sth** pay for sth as a present to sb – 7 **jolt** shock – 13 **sleeping pad** *(AE)* mat, thick piece of soft material

Heading down the path toward the exit, I found myself behind a construction worker with an orange hard hat and a lunch pail.

Even though I had the booklet of tickets for the town bus, I wasn't sure which to take and decided to walk the two miles to school. The sun was just starting to come up when I got there and the sensation of hunger had awakened in my stomach. The front doors were locked, but I knew the janitors used the side entrance behind the Dumpsters. Inside, the halls were empty and dim. My footsteps echoed on the tiles as I headed to the gym.

With shampoo, soap, and deodorant already in my gym locker, I showered.

A little while later I was leaving the locker room when Coach Buder came in. When he saw me, a scowl etched its way onto his narrow, lined face.

"Here early," he said.

I nodded, not feeling like I had to explain. After being coached by him through four years of baseball, I still felt like I hardly knew him. He was retiring after this year and sometimes I got the feeling that he'd had enough of high school sports.

"Everything on track for Rice?" he asked as he unzipped his athletic jacket.

I nodded. "Just have to sign the letter of intent."

"How's the arm?"

"Still there."

He smiled. "You deserve it, Dan. You're probably the most talented player to ever come through here, not to mention one of the hardest working."

"Thanks, coach."

"Stay on track now, you hear?"

2 **pail** *(AE)* small container – 8 **Dumpster** container for rubbish (trademarked name) – 14 **scowl** facial expression of dislike – 21 **on track** *(here)* ok – 23 **letter of intent** written statement expressing the intention of the writer to sign a contract

"Definitely," I replied, but at the same time I wondered why he'd said that. Did he somehow sense that I was in danger of falling off track?

Coach Buder nodded in a way that meant the conversation was over. He'd done his duty and dispensed his coachly advice. Now he could go into his office and dream about retiring to Florida or whatever his plan was. Some of the guys called him Buddha behind his back because he had that detached way about him. Even though I'd only met Coach Petersen from Rice once, I'd spoken to him a lot on the phone, and already felt closer to him than I ever had to Buddha.

By lunchtime I was starving. When it comes to bargains the school lunch is pretty cheap, but the portions are small. On the menu that day was a chicken leg over rice, cauliflower and peas, and applesauce.

Being the best pitcher on the team, I'd been written about in the school and local papers, so the lunch ladies knew who I was. I always made a point of saying hello and asking how they were. When you play team sports, you learn that what a player does off the field can be just as important as what he or she does on it. You represent your town and school, and if you make it big someday, you'll want the folks back home to say nice things about you. That day Lisa, a skinny blonde with a gravelly smoker's voice, was behind the counter.

"Think I could have a little more?" I asked when I saw how skimpy that drumstick was.

"You can buy another main course, honey," she said.

I knew I could, but that would nearly double the cost of lunch and Mom had portioned out the lunch money for one meal per day. So taking a second main course now would mean not having enough at the end of the month. "Thanks. I probably shouldn't."

8 **detached** reserved, distant – 23 **gravelly** harsh – 26 **skimpy** little – 26 **drumstick** the lower part of the leg of a chicken

Lisa looked puzzled. "It doesn't cost that much."

"Yeah, I know. Thanks anyway." I slid my tray toward the cashier. They say it's the little things that count, and I was beginning to see that part of being homeless was not being able to count on the little things, like an extra helping of school lunch. I'd just given the cashier my PIN when Lisa came over with a second helping of chicken and rice in a Styrofoam bowl.

"Here you go, honey," she said, and gave the cashier a knowing wink.

"Hey, thanks." My growling stomach appreciated it, but my head felt uncomfortable. Would this be my life from now on? Sneaking into school early to take showers, and depending on handouts at lunch?

As I headed for the table where the usual suspects were sitting, I wondered if it was possible that Lisa had given me the extra food because she'd somehow heard about my family moving to Dignityville. No, it wasn't possible. Not yet. But how long would it be before the whole school knew?

"Looks like someone's hungry," Noah quipped when I put my tray down. Talia smiled at me and turned back to her conversation with Tory. She'd gone with her family to their lake house for the weekend. We'd stayed in touch, mostly texting, but I hadn't been able to bring myself to tell her about our latest move.

One thing was certain: I wouldn't be able to avoid it for long.

***

By the afternoon I'd really begun to drag. The combination of not getting much sleep the previous night and getting up so early that morning had caught up to me. Back in the day I'd kept a couple of Red Bulls in my locker for moments like this, but when money got tight, I'd let that lapse.

2 **to slide, slid** to move slowly – 12 **to sneak into** to enter secretly – 27 **to drag** *here:* be very tired – 31 **to lapse** to come to an end

"Think it's time to get the arm loose?" Noah asked in the weight room after school while we worked out with kettlebells. Every fall after summer showcase ball ended, I rested my arm for two months and focused on core and leg strength.

"Why?"

He cocked his head curiously. "Uh ... because the Fall Classic is coming up and maybe you ought to prepare for it?"

"Oh, yeah." I yawned and started another set of swings with the bells. To be honest, I hadn't thought much about the tournament for the past few days. There'd been other things on my mind. Noah and I agreed that I should probably start throwing at our next workout, and then we went back to core training.

"Need a ride?" he asked later when we left the gym.

I'd known this moment was coming, but my sleep-deprived brain hadn't figured out how to handle it. Now it was here. I probably should have made up some excuse for walking home, but I was so bushed that I really did want that ride.

When I didn't answer, Noah frowned. "What's with you?"

There was no way around it."We moved over the weekend."

"Again? Where?"

I stopped walking. We were in the parking lot. The afternoon had turned chilly and you could smell fall in the fresh, dry breeze. I started to say, *Swear you won't tell anyone,* but caught myself. Who was I kidding? Sooner or later everyone would know.

Noah waited with a puzzled expression on his face.

"Dignityville." No matter what Aubrey said about being a pioneer in a new way of living, it felt humiliating to hear those words come out of my mouth. I, Dan Halprin, was officially homeless.

Noah looked down at the asphalt and crushed a dry brown leaf with his shoe. "Sorry, man."

2 **to work out** to do physical exercises – 2 **kettlebell** *Kugelhantel* – 3 **showcase ball** summer camp where high school baseball players learn from top coaches – 9 **bell** see above (kettlebell) – 18 **to be bushed** *(inf)* to be extremely tired, exhausted

"Me too."

We got into his car and I told him how Dad and Uncle Ron had never gotten along, and how Mom couldn't take the stressful, negative atmosphere in that house.

"Told Tal?" Noah asked.

"Not yet."

He shot me a look like, *Are you serious?*

"Yeah, yeah, I know."

"You don't want her to find out from someone else," he advised. "I don't want her to find out, period," I muttered, once again feeling something that I'd been trying really, really hard to resist: anger and resentment … not at Talia, not at the world, but at my parents.

It was thanks to them that I was suffering this embarrassment.

We drove the rest of the way in silence. But when we got into town I couldn't go straight back to Dignityville. "That's good." I pointed at a Starbucks.

"Free Wi-Fi?" Noah guessed, pulling over.

"You got it. Thanks for the ride."

Noah drummed his fingers on the steering wheel and gave me a grave look. "If there's anything I can do, you know?"

"Thanks, man."

"Need a lift in the morning?" he asked.

When we'd lived a half-dozen blocks from each other, getting rides to and from school was no big deal, especially since Noah and I were on the same schedule. But giving me a ride now would mean going miles out of his way.

"I can manage," I said.

"On what? The bus?" He knew how much I hated riding with the middle schoolers. And I had yet to figure out if the public system went anywhere near school.

"Since when do you get up any earlier than you have to?" I asked.

"Hey, ain't no biggie, white boy."

34 **ain't no biggie** *(sl)* it's no big deal

13

It wasn't easy to sit in Starbucks and do my homework. I'd had one meal that day–lunch–and I was starving. The brownies and muffins called out to me, and the scent of coffee just made it worse.

Plus, I was trying to deal with all this stupid internal strife. Alternately feeling angry at my parents for dragging me to Dignityville, and then feeling guilty for being angry at them.

Why couldn't Dad have kept just one of those jobs he'd started and lost in the past year?

Even if Mom couldn't find another job as a stockbroker, couldn't she have gotten work doing something else?

But she wasn't happy in that world. ...

Yeah, well, I was not happy in *this* world. ...

It wasn't quite dark when I left Starbucks, and I was famished. In Dignityville the dining tent was crowded, but I passed it and went to my own tent instead. Mom was inside, lying on her sleeping bag, reading *The Zen of Gardening* in the lantern light. The sweet, perfumed scent in the air meant she'd burned incense to get rid of the musty smell.

"There you are," she said. "Have you eaten? You must be starved."

"Want to go over and get me something?" I asked.

Mom closed the book and sat up. "You can't avoid it, sweetheart. Now come on, I've been waiting for you."

"What about Dad?"

"He's out somewhere."

I didn't want to go into the dining tent, but it looked like I had no choice. Maybe it didn't matter. I was still living in Dignityville whether I ate there or not.

It was warm and humid inside the Grand Ballroom. People of all ages–couples, families with kids, and old folks–were chowing down. Just like at school I picked up a tray and a plastic

5 **strife** conflict – 14 **famished** very hungry – 18 **incense** aromatic substance

knife and fork, and got in line. The woman in front of me was wearing a city bus driver's uniform. It still seemed weird that you could have a job and yet be homeless, but I had a feeling it was just one more thing about this new world that people had to get used to.

Dinner was spaghetti and meatballs, salad, and bread and butter. Pony-tailed Wade was one of the people who served us, and I remembered him saying that everyone at Dignityville took turns serving or cleaning up. Our trays full, Mom and I found an empty table. It's strange how the hungrier you are, the better everything tastes. The spaghetti was pretty good, and the meatballs were tasty enough to make me wonder if I could go back for more. Lucky for me, Mom being a vegetarian, gave me hers.

"Feel like company?" Meg and Aubrey approached our table. Even though he looked older, I wondered if they were a couple. Meg smiled as if, now that I was also living in Dignityville, she was willing to forgive me for that humiliating scene in that empty classroom the week before.

"Please do," Mom said.

"I thought you looked familiar, Dan." Aubrey set his tray down. "Meg told me you pitch for the school and I realized I've seen you. You've got great stuff."

"Thanks." There'd once been a baseball player called Shoeless Joe Jackson. Maybe someday I'd be known as Homeless Dan Halprin.

Aubrey turned to Mom. "We're going to need the town's approval for that garden. Maybe we could work on the proposal after dinner? And I think it would be really helpful if you went to the meeting at Town Hall this Friday and spoke about how beneficial it would be, and how it would save the town money. That's really what they want to hear."

24 **Shoeless Joe Jackson** Joseph Jefferson Jackson (1887–1951) nicknamed Shoeless Joe because he once took off his uncomfortable shoes during a match – 31 **beneficial** having a good effect

He turned to me. "So, Dan, how's it going?"

"Okay," I lied.

Aubrey narrowed one eye as if he knew I wasn't being sincere. "Listen, it takes a while. And even then this place isn't for everyone."

Mom nodded in agreement. "Just give it a chance, sweetheart."

"Anything else on your mind?" Aubrey asked.

There was: "Any part-time work around here? Like on the weekends?"

Aubrey pressed his lips together thoughtfully. "It's all on a voluntary basis here. No one gets paid."

"I meant, like, in town?" I said.

"Unskilled labor?"

"Uh-huh."

He shrugged. "There's not much, and a lot of people are vying for what there is. Some guys check the bulletin boards at the post office and supermarkets every morning. You just have to get lucky."

"You have a job?" I asked.

"I told you he did," Meg said.

Huh? When had she and I talked about Aubrey?

"Remember that day at my locker?" she said. "I told you both my mom and brother had jobs."

Brother? I guess I must have looked surprised, because Aubrey chuckled and put his hand on Meg's head. "Meet my little sister."

"Gotcha."

We were joined by Joel, the heavyset guy with the bushy beard who we'd met two days ago. "Aubrey, we gotta talk about the bikes."

"Sure." Aubrey got up to leave, then paused as if he'd just thought of something. "Know Ruby's Bar and Grill on the other side of town, just off Main Street? Why don't you swing by there

13 **unskilled labor** work for which you don't need any qualifications – 15 **to vie** [vaɪ] to compete very hard

around five on Wednesday? We'll talk to my boss. He might have a job for you."

After he left, I turned to Meg. "Nice guy."

"*Great* guy," said Meg. "Of course, I'm biased, but he really cares. And he's trying to do something. "

"What's that about bikes?" Mom asked.

"They're starting a bike drive," Meg said. "You know how they have coat and food drives? This'll make it easier for the people here to get around town."

Mom finished dinner and went back to our tent. Left alone with Meg, I felt a nagging sensation. "So ... about the other day in that classroom, I–"

"It's okay," she cut me short. "What goes on between you and your girlfriend is none of my business."

"Yeah, but it made me think," I said.

Meg feigned a wide-eyed, astonished look. "Really?"

"Why do you have to be such a wise guy?" I asked with a smile.

Meg smiled back, but before she could reply, an argument broke out in the TV area at the back of the tent. A couple of old guys were growling at each other, probably about what show to watch.

"Hard to believe." Meg sighed. "One day you're just like everyone else with a house in a nice town, and the next day ..."

"You're a pioneer in a new, bold experiment in living?" I finished the sentence.

She gave me a sour look.

"You don't buy it?" I asked, surprised."But he's your brother."

"Sometimes I buy it," she said. "And sometimes ... I sit in that tent and think, 'How can this be happening?'"

I raised my hand, palm out, and she slapped it.

"Do your friends know?" I asked.

4 **biased** prejudiced, one-sided – 16 **to feign** [feɪn] to make up, pretend *(vortäuschen)* – 27 **you don't buy it?** *(sl)* you don't accept it as true?

"Only a few," Meg said. "We didn't move to Median until I started high school, so I don't have all that many friends. But *you*, on the other hand ..."

If Meg knew the truth, she would have been surprised. I was "friendly" with lots of people, but there was only a handful that I was really tight with.

We stayed at the table in the dining tent and talked about school, friends, homelessness, and life in general. To be honest, by the time we'd finished, I couldn't say I felt one bit better about being in Dignityville, but having Meg there did make it feel a little more bearable.

6 **tight** *(inf)* close friends with

14

I resolved to tell Talia about Dignityville the next day after lunch. But when I came out of the lunch line and sat down, she pressed her lips close to my ear and whispered, "When were you going to tell me?"

"Never?" I whispered back.

The faint lines in her forehead deepened ever so slightly. She didn't get the joke. But maybe she wasn't supposed to. I let out a long sigh to let her know that I didn't need to be interrogated at the lunch table in front of our friends, but Talia either didn't get it or didn't care.

"So what happens now?" she whispered.

"With what?" I asked.

"You're not going to stay there, are you?"

There's a deep sinking, regretful sensation you get when the bases are loaded and you give up a grand slam. I'd thought that feeling was limited to baseball.

Can you believe Talia Purcellen's boyfriend is living in that tent city for homeless people?

Poor Talia. How humiliating!

I could have said something nasty. Maybe, *Sorry if it messes up your social life.* But that would have been my own anger and frustration leaking out.

Talia started to say something more, then stopped and glanced at Tory as if she could feel her trying to listen in on our conversation. More than anyone else in our crowd, Tory was the great social arbiter, whose say about what we did and who we did it with carried more weight than anyone else's.

I motioned to Talia that if she wanted to keep talking we should go somewhere else. When we rose from the table, Tory's eyes narrowed with disapproval.

15 **bases loaded** baseball term meaning there are runners on first, second, and third base – 15 **grand slam** in baseball a home run hit with all three bases occupied by baserunners, thus scoring four runs, the most possible in one play – 26 **arbiter** *(here)* authority

We went out to the courtyard and sat on a bench. It was chilly and Talia hugged herself. "Your dad's still looking for a job, isn't he?"

Was she trying to come up with the explanations she imagined she'd need when our friends asked about me being homeless?

"Oh, yeah," I said, although he'd probably have better luck panning for gold in the muddy stream that ran behind Dignityville. Jobs running sports programs for poor inner-city kids no longer existed. The government couldn't afford them anymore. But even that wasn't the whole story. Like Mom, Dad just seemed to be giving up.

Talia hunched over and squeezed her hands between her knees as if some invisible weight was pressing down on her. She might have even been fighting back tears. Someone else might have given her grief for thinking only of herself. But that wasn't fair. When I'd started dating her it wasn't because of her politics or great humanitarian endeavors. It was because she was a hot, popular chick. And she'd started dating me because I was a popular, studly jock.

Not a popular studly *homeless* jock.

"Listen, Tal, it's not like we lost our house on purpose."

She nodded. "But you … you can't just *stay* there." It was like she couldn't accept it. Like this wasn't the reality she felt entitled to.

Even though we were outside, I dropped my voice. "Seriously? I didn't *decide* to become homeless, and my parents didn't *decide* to lose their jobs. I mean, maybe a little understanding is in order, don't you think?"

Talia nodded, but didn't look at me. Her mood seemed so forlorn that I added, "It's not like someone died."

She worked a jagged smile onto her face, but kept her eyes averted. I could tell she wasn't buying it.

7 **to pan for gold** to rinse soil in order to separate gold from dirt – 12 **to hunch over** to bend over – 17 **endeavor** act, deed, effort – 18 **chick** *(inf, sl)* attractive girl – 19 **studly jock** *(inf, sl)* attractive, young, male athlete

Oh, great. My parents lose their jobs and we lose our home. And now I'm going to lose my girlfriend.

I put my arm around her shoulders. "Come on, Tal, how do you think it makes me feel when you act like me living in Dignityville is so horrible?"

She sniffed."I'm sorry, Dan. It's … just not what I expected."

"Well … believe me, that makes two of us."

15

That afternoon Noah and I went out to the field behind school and started throwing. Not pitching, just lobbing the ball back and forth as we began the process of getting my arm loose after not pitching for two months. It was a warm, sunny afternoon and might have been enjoyable had I not had the twin burdens of homelessness and Talia.

We'd probably been throwing for about fifteen minutes when Tyler Buchholz and Zach Raines strolled out. Tyler was our first baseman and probably the best hitter on the team. He'd also been invited to the Thanksgiving tournament.

"How's the arm feel?" Zach set down his backpack and unzipped it.

"Pretty good," I said. "At least nothing hurts."

"Hear that?" Zach said to Tyler, who'd wandered behind me to look at something.

"Yeah," I heard Tyler answer. "Always a good sign when nothing hurts."

The next thing I knew, a pair of arms went around me from behind.

"Hey!" I yelled, more annoyed than panicked since I knew it had to be Tyler.

Zach pulled what looked like a blue bathrobe out of his backpack and threw it over my head. Everything went dark … blue. "What the …?"

Tyler had my arms pinned to my sides. Now I felt something like a belt go around me as Zach tied the robe closed. "Be cool, Dan. We're doing this for your own good."

"Resistance is futile," I heard Noah add. They started to guide me … back toward the school, I assumed.

"Guys, you don't have to kidnap me," I said calmly as they led me across the grass. "I'll go wherever you want."

"Not if you knew where you're going," Noah replied ominously.

2 **to lob** to throw gently and high in the air – 28 **futile** ['fjuːt̬əl] pointless, useless

When we stepped down from a curb, I knew we were in the parking lot. A car door opened and they guided me into the backseat and buckled the seat belt. They sat on either side of me in case I tried to squirm out from under the robe.

"You don't think someone may notice that you've got a guy tied up in the backseat?" I asked when the car began to move.

"We'll take our chances," Noah replied from the front.

We didn't go far. When they helped me out of the car, I could hear traffic and had a feeling we were at a strip mall. We went through a door and the scent of burgers and fries wafted into my nose. I could hear bits of conversations and some chuckling as the guys led me to a seat. Surely they'd take the robe off my head now, wouldn't they?

Nope. Instead, dishes clattered, soda fizzed as it was poured into glasses, and something scraped the tabletop.

Whispers and girlish giggling followed. Now I thought I knew what was up. They'd taken me to Wally's Wowza-Burger and the girls were all there for a "Let's Cheer Up Homeless Dan" party. *Whoop dee doo!*

"Ready?" I heard Noah ask.

Some female voices answered yes and I was just registering the fact that they weren't *familiar* female voices when the robe was pulled off and I found myself staring at a huge platter of chicken wings with a candle on top.

Wally's didn't serve chicken wings.

I raised my eyes. On the other side of the table half a dozen smiling Hooters girls in tight T-shirts and shorts started clapping and singing the Hooters birthday song.

And just like that, Homeless Dan cheered up.

"I had to tell them it was your birthday," Noah said later while he drove me home. "It was the only way I could get them to sing."

1 **curb** edge of the road between the sidewalk and the street – 27 **Hooters** a restaurant chain serving fast food

"Thanks, man." I punched him playfully in the arm. He was a solid friend … something I really needed right now.

Back "home" in the tent I found Mom cutting Dad's hair. He was sitting with a towel around his shoulders while she snipped with a pair of office shears.

"Since when do you cut hair?" I asked, feeling the cheerful glow of the Hooters party quickly dissipate now that I was back in the last place I wanted to be.

"It's not that hard." Mom squeezed a lock of Dad's hair between her fingers and carefully trimmed the end.

When she finished cutting, she lathered the back of Dad's neck and shaved it, then carefully removed the towel so Dad's hair didn't fall on the tent floor. I had to admit that she'd done a pretty decent job.

"Next?" She swept her arm toward the empty folding chair.

She was right. Maybe I was more sensitive than usual about looking scruffy. Would people look at me and think, *Oh, yeah, that's the homeless kid. Probably can't afford a haircut?*

I sat down.

"Buzz cut?" Mom joked.

"Just a trim, thanks."

Dad decided to take a shower. When he took off his shirt, I noticed a small wad of gauze taped to the inside of his forearm.

"You okay?" I asked.

He seemed puzzled. "Sure. Why?"

I nodded at his arm.

He looked surprised, as if he'd forgotten about the gauze. "Oh, yeah. It's nothing."

"Just a checkup?"

"Right."

***

Our Dignityville neighbors were Mona and her young daughter, Stella, who went to day care on the days her mom worked as a

7 **to dissipate** to go away, to vanish – 11 **to lather** ['læðər] to put soap or shaving cream on – 20 **buzz cut** short hairstyle – 21 **trim** minor cut, to make hair look neater

cashier at Home Depot. On the other side were Fred and Diane, an older couple with a strangely upbeat attitude considering what their lives had been reduced to. Diane was gray-haired and plump. Fred was a skinny bald guy with a pointy Adam's apple who always had a lame joke to tell. It seemed like they spent most of their week waiting for the weekends, when they'd babysit their grandchildren.

"You going to the meeting at Town Hall on Friday?" Fred asked after dinner that night.

Mom nodded. "Aubrey put the proposal for the garden on the agenda."

"How do you make an artichoke?" Fred asked.

"Steam it?" said Mom.

"No, strangle it." Fred grinned.

"Oh, Fred." Whenever her husband told a corny joke, Diane would slap him lightly on the shoulder and they'd both giggle like a couple of kids.

They were homeless. How could they be so jolly?

2 **upbeat** *(inf)* cheerful – 15 **corny** unoriginal, banal

16

Ruby's Bar and Grill was fancier than the name might have implied. The brass door handle was polished and the velvet drapes were a deep, rich maroon. Inside I almost didn't recognize Aubrey behind the bar. His hair was slicked back and he was wearing a white shirt and dark vest.

The bar was half-full and he motioned me down to the end where we could speak in private.

His smile was genuine. "What'll it be? Martini? Manhattan?"

"Job?"

He grinned. "Victor's out for a few minutes, but I told him you were coming by." He poured a Coke with ice and slid it in front of me. "How's it going?"

All I could do was shrug. Aubrey nodded as if he understood. "Listen, man, I know it's impossible not to take what's happening to you personally, but sometimes a little perspective helps, okay? It's not your parents' fault, and it's not the government's fault. Downturns have always been part of the economic landscape. But they don't last forever. Things'll turn around. Don't forget, you've got a long life ahead of you."

"Someday we'll look back at all this and laugh?" I asked with sour humor.

"I sure hope not." Aubrey poured himself a Coke. "Hopefully, we've learned a lesson. And because of it, we'll change things so that the next time something like this happens, there'll be safety nets to catch people before they slide all the way down to Dignityville."

"But if things are going to get better, why make Dignityville permanent?"

With a finger, Aubrey wiped some condensation off the glass. When he looked up at me, some of the brightness had left his eyes. "Things will get better *someday* ... because they always do.

3 **maroon** dark red

But it may take a while. And by the time it happens, it may be too late for some people. They may not have the education or skills for the jobs of the future."

A short, bald man in a neatly pressed suit joined us, and Aubrey made the introductions. He was Victor, the manager of Ruby's.

"Aubrey tells me you're responsible and a hard worker," he said in a gruff voice. We talked while Aubrey left to serve some customers. I guess I made a good impression, because Victor said that if I could wait until after Thanksgiving, there'd be a busboy's job for me.

I told him I could wait, and thanked him gratefully. By now people were coming in after work and Aubrey was too busy serving drinks to chat. He waved good-bye and said we'd catch up later.

I left Ruby's in a state of semishock. Aubrey hardly knew me and couldn't possibly have known that I was responsible or a hard worker, and yet he'd put his word on the line to help me get that job. What an outstanding guy.

The following afternoon Noah couldn't work out because he had to help Derek move a new soundboard into the studio. Talia had one of her after-school meetings, and I figured I'd study in the media center and wait for her.

It didn't occur to me that her meeting would be in one of the small glass-enclosed rooms that ran along one side of the library, but there she was, along with Tory, Ben, and a few others.

And, from the expressions on their faces, it was obvious that they weren't having fun. I stood on the other side of the media center and watched what appeared to be a heated argument.

Ben looked up and saw me through the glass. Inside the room, he said something and instantly Tory and Talia swiveled around and stared. It might have been self-centered to think that

10 **busboy** waiter's helper – 17 **put his word on the line** stated his personal confidence in sb as reliable

whatever they were discussing had something to do with me, but from the way they were acting, it was hard to think otherwise.

Almost as quickly as they'd swiveled to look at me, the girls swung back and began talking again. A lot of head-shaking and anguished expressions followed and I figured I better turn my attention to schoolwork. I was just about to sit down at a table when the meeting room door opened and Talia waved at me to join them.

It seemed strange that they'd want me in their meeting, and only got stranger when everyone in the room except Tory, Talia, and Ben left. Talia closed the door and we sat. I couldn't imagine what was going on. An awkward moment passed and then Talia said, "Dan, how would you feel about a scholarship to the winter formal?"

I frowned. A scholarship to a school dance? I'd never heard of such a thing. Then the jarring realization hit home. "For me?"

Ben let out an exasperated sigh. "I'm sorry, Dan. I'm trying to explain to them that we can't do it." He turned to the girls. "You can't create a scholarship just so you can give it to a friend."

"What if it's based on need?" Talia asked.

"Then you have to consider everyone else who might qualify," Ben said. "Now you're talking about people applying for it based on financial need. They'd have to present financial statements, bank accounts, all sorts of stuff. And you'd have to go through it all, and if the scholarship went to Dan everyone would *still* think it had been created just for him."

It wasn't hard to get the picture. The least expensive thing about the winter formal is the ticket to the dance. There's also the tux rental, the party bus or limo, the after-party club, and on and on. It probably wasn't that Talia didn't want to pay for me, as much as she didn't want the whole school to know.

13 **scholarship** amount of money given to sb to help their education – 13 **winter formal** dance held by high school *(Winterfest)* – 16 **jarring** disturbing – 29 **tux** *(abb for* **tuxedo** complete, formal suit outfit worn by men to important parties in the US

It made me incredibly uncomfortable. “Thanks, guys, but I can’t accept charity.”

“What about your scholarship to Rice?” Talia asked.

“I earned that by pitching.”

“Not to mention what they’ll earn on ticket sales, merchandise, and TV deals,” Ben added.

Talia began to argue. “But–”

“Talia!” I didn’t mean to raise my voice as sharply as it came out. Talia instantly hunched her shoulders and went quiet. Suddenly none of them could look me in the eye.

“Ben, you’re totally right. There’s no way I’d accept this.” I turned to Talia and put my hand on her arm. “Listen, I appreciate what you were trying to do, but … it’s just … try to see it from my point of view. That’s not the kind of attention I need.”

She nodded mutely.

Tory cleared her throat. “We have a lot more that we need to discuss here, Dan, so maybe …”

“I hear you,” I said, and left.

Talia and I had a long talk that night. She started off upset and defensive–insisting she’d only been trying to help–but I got her to calm down by telling her I appreciated it, and then repeating that I didn’t want to do anything that singled me out. Eventually Talia said she understood, and the topic of the winter formal was left unresolved.

On Friday night Mom and Dad went to Town Hall after dinner. The whole weekend lay ahead and I was wondering what to do. Talia and her mom had planned a bunch of college visits, so she’d be away. At Dignityville a group gathered each evening to watch the TV at the back of the dining tent, but I couldn’t picture myself among them. Then I spotted Meg and an older woman coming up the path between the rows of tents. The woman’s

15 **mutely** silently

hair was curly gray, but her skin wasn't as wrinkled as you might have expected. She got closer and I began to see the resemblance and knew she was Mrs. Fine.

They stopped and Meg introduced us.

"Meg's told me about you," Mrs. Fine said, and gave her daughter a kind of amused smile as if they knew something I didn't know. Then she said to Meg, "Not too late tonight, okay?"

Meg nodded. Her mom said it was nice to meet me and left.

"What was that smile about?" I asked.

"That you thought I was Aubrey's girlfriend."

"Hey, it was a natural mistake. Anyone could have made it."

"I know. We just had a laugh." She gave me a curious look. "Whatcha up to?"

"Not much. You?"

"Aubrey asked me to go to the town council meeting. He's bartending tonight."

"Think something's going to happen?" I asked.

"We never know. He's always worried they might try to sneak a motion through that will hurt Dignityville, so if I see something like that happening, I'm supposed to call him." She paused and studied me. "Want to come?"

I can't say I was thrilled. Going to that meeting sounded like as much fun as doing the crab walk in gym, but at least it would pass the time.

We sat in the last row. Not only had I never been to a city council meeting, I'd never been to Town Hall. The room was more than half-full when the council came in and sat at a panel in the front. Mayor George, a heavy, red-faced man, sat behind a plaque that said council president. Three women and three men sat beside him.

18 **to sneak a motion through** to put in a formal proposal secretly – 23 **crab walk** an intense upper body and core exercise that uses your own bodyweight for resistance

The meeting started with the Pledge of Allegiance and some reports on various town projects. It wasn't long before I leaned over to Meg and whispered, "Boring."

"It's government," she whispered back. "It's *supposed* to be boring."

I wasn't sure if she was trying to be funny, or just stating a basic fact. Either way, I was seriously considering leaving when Mayor George asked for comments about a proposal to add permanent toilet facilities to the washing area at Dignityville.

Chair legs scraped in the middle of the crowd and Uncle Ron stood up. I'd had no idea he was there, and from the looks I caught on my parents' faces when they swiveled to see who was speaking, it was pretty obvious they hadn't either. I slid down in my seat to make sure they didn't see me in the back of the room.

"Mayor, I'd like to speak for all the residents who are sick and tired of seeing our town turned into a dumping ground for bums," Uncle Ron began forcefully. "I'd also like to remind the council that when it approved this incredibly bad idea of turning a public park into a camp for the homeless, it did so with the understanding that it would be on a temporary basis. Now it looks more and more like you want to make it a permanent part of our community. I don't have to tell you what this is doing to our property values and to the reputation of our town in general."

A bunch of people in the audience clapped, and you could see that Mayor George wasn't happy. Meg leaned close and whispered, "This is what Aubrey's worried about."

"Think you should call him?" I whispered back.

"Maybe. Let's see."

Mayor George leaned forward. "We are not trying to make it a permanent facility."

Mutters of disbelief and disapproval flitted through the crowd. I was starting to get the feeling that most of those attending were against Dignityville.

1 **Pledge of Allegiance** expression of loyalty to the flag of the United States and the republic of the United States of America

"But you just said you're planning to remove the portable restrooms and replace them with permanent toilet facilities," Uncle Ron pointed out.

"Strictly as a cost savings," replied Mayor George. "It's my understanding that the sewer lines can be easily disconnected when and if the homeless problem decreases."

For confirmation he glanced at the town engineer, who nodded.

"*If* the homeless problem decreases?" Uncle Ron repeated angrily. "How many times do I have to remind you that erecting that camp and now improving the facilities isn't going to *decrease* the problem. It's only going to make it worse!"

More applause. You could feel the animosity in the crowd. It was like playing an away game at the school of our arch-enemies.

"I'd like to point out that Dignityville has been open for almost four months and we've had no indication that anyone has moved in from another community," the mayor replied.

"Just wait until they hear about the improvements you're making," Uncle Ron shot back.

"Yeah!" someone in the crowd agreed loudly, and other people nodded.

Once again Mayor George leaned forward. "I'd like to remind *all of you* that the town council's mandate is to act on behalf of the *entire* community and not just for the benefit of a few individuals like yourselves. We have a significant homeless problem here in Median and it is our responsibility to care for them while they try to get back on their feet."

A few people booed, and someone shouted, "If they really wanted jobs they'd either go get them or start a business!"

"I say we have a recall vote and elect a new mayor!" yelled someone else.

5 **sewer** ['suːɔr] pipe or underground drain used to carry away waste water – 23 **mandate** official duty given to you by other people (*here:* by voters) – 30 **recall** removal of a public official by vote

"Thank you for your opinions," Mayor George replied tersely. "We're going to move on to other business."

More grumbles of disapproval followed. His face flushed with frustration, Uncle Ron was about to sit when he saw Mom and Dad near the front. From his surprised expression, it was obvious that he'd had no idea they were there.

Meanwhile Mayor George studied the papers in front of him. "Up next is a proposal to turn approximately three thousand square feet of Osborne Park into a vegetable garden for the benefit of those living there."

He looked up with a woeful expression, as if he knew he was about to catch serious grief. "Any comments?"

More mutters of disapproval bubbled up from the crowd, but Mom was the only one who raised her hand. I felt proud when she stood up and turned so that she was speaking to the crowd as well as the council. "I'd just like to say a few things. First, the vegetable garden will save the town money because the residents will eat what they grow. This will also help them have a healthier diet, which should cut down on medical costs. In addition there'll be certain times of the year when we'll probably grow more than we'll be able to consume, and we can sell the surplus at the farmer's market and use the money to pay for fertilizer, farming tools, and other expenses. Finally, a garden will be beneficial because it will give the residents a reason to be active. As a resident of Dignityville myself, I've seen firsthand that one of the problems is that not everyone has enough to–"

"They could be looking for jobs!" a man snarled loudly, and a large part of the crowd clapped.

Mom set her jaw firmly. "Many of them already *have* jobs," she snapped. "And some of those who don't have been looking *for years*. And if you've ever been unemployed, you know how disheartening that can be."

11 **woeful** [ˈwoʊfəl] sorrowful, unhappy – 22 **fertilizer** substance that makes plants grow – 32 **disheartening** demoralising

I felt like clapping, but didn't want to attract attention to myself. I think some of the crowd was caught off guard by how ardent and unafraid Mom was. She gathered herself and then continued more calmly. "As I was saying, when they're *not* looking for jobs, they would have something rewarding to do instead of sitting around watching TV. This garden won't cost the town anything, and there'll be nothing permanent about it. When the time comes to dismantle Dignityville, they'll just plow it under, seed it with grass, and it'll be a park again."

A couple of people muttered under their breath, but no one rose to argue. Mom thanked the council and sat.

Mayor George held a vote. The vegetable garden was approved four to three.

The meeting ended and people began to leave. Uncle Ron was coming down the aisle when Meg and I stood up. When he saw us, he looked perplexed, as if embarrassed to have spoken so harshly against the place where we were now living. I decided to make it easier for him. "How are the twins?"

He appeared to relax. "Still getting into mischief," he said, then added, "They ask about you."

"I'll try to get over there," I said.

"They'd like that." He glanced toward the front of the room, where Mom and Dad were speaking with the town engineer. "How're you doing?"

"Hanging in. Having that garden'll make Mom happy."

Uncle Ron's nose twitched. It was weird. Here we were, family, but also enemies. *Famenies.* He sighed, nodded, and continued down the aisle.

"You know him?" Meg asked, not hiding her surprise.

"He's my mother's brother."

"*That* man is your uncle?" she said, astonished. "Why's he so against Dignityville?"

3 **ardent** enthusiastic – 8 **to dismantle** to take apart – 19 **mischief** trouble

I explained that he was a real estate lawyer and had some half-finished condominiums that no one wanted. "I think he's got some pretty serious financial problems."

Meg didn't reply. As we left Town Hall and started back toward Dignityville, I felt kind of weird, because in a way Uncle Ron was right. Aubrey did envision Dignityville becoming permanent. While that would be good for the homeless in town, there would be others, like Ron, who might be hurt.

Suddenly a hand grabbed my arm. "Dan?"

We'd gotten to a busy corner. The light was red.

"Were you going to stop?" Meg gave me a concerned look.

I wasn't even aware that we'd been about to cross the street. "Thanks," I said.

"Are you okay?"

No, not even close.

17

A PHONE CALL

"I'd like your help."

"How?"

"I need to get in touch with a certain kind of person. I think you might know how to do that."

"What kind of person?"

"Someone I could pay to do something."

"Like what?"

"That doesn't concern you."

"Why should I help you?"

"Because if you do, then I'll help you. You do understand how I could help you?"

Silence.

"Did you hear what I just said?"

"Yes, I think so."

"Good. So are you willing to put me in touch with the kind of person I need?"

"I'll think about it."

"I wouldn't think too long if I were you."

18

I hated to admit it, but I was relieved that Talia was away that weekend and not around to remind me of all the things I couldn't afford to do. Instead I worked: *out* with Noah, *for* Ron's neighbor, and *on* my studies.

Sunday evening was my turn to do after-dinner cleanup in the Grand Ballroom. When I got to the dining tent, the volunteers had begun serving dinner, but Mom and Stella were playing Chutes and Ladders. Mom was beaming and you could see how much delight she took in having a little girl to look after.

"Shouldn't we get in line?" I asked.

"Go ahead. Stella and I haven't finished our game."

With her dark eyes Stella looked up at me. "I'm going to win. And this time Hannah isn't letting me."

"I've never let you win," Mom protested.

"You did once," Stella said accusingly.

"Okay, maybe once," Mom admitted. "But not this time, young lady."

Stella grinned devilishly. "And I'm still going to beat you."

I didn't know Stella's precise age, but I would have guessed she was about five. Mona, her mom, had worked for a solar panel company until they moved their manufacturing to China. Now she had a job at Home Depot during the day and was a waitress a few nights a week. I assumed that's where she was that night while Mom watched her daughter.

It was hard to imagine what it must have been like, being five and growing up in a camp for homeless people. There were a couple of kids around who looked like they were twelve or thirteen, but I was pretty sure I hadn't seen anyone as young as Stella. No kids her age to play with. No playdates. And it wasn't

22 **Home Depot** chain of home improvement shops, supplying tools, construction products, and services

like the folks who spent their days watching TV in the back of the dining tent were going to let her watch cartoons.

At school Lisa, the lunch lady, made a habit of slipping me extra food, but I only took advantage of the offer when I'd missed breakfast or was really hungry. I guess we'd gotten a little lackadaisical about it, though, because the day came when I was in line and she said, "Need a little extra today, honey?"

"Yeah, thanks." I hadn't bought breakfast that morning because the weekend was coming and I wanted to hold on to whatever money I had for going out.

Lisa had just given me some extra chicken nuggets and tater tots when the next guy in line said, "Can I have some extra too?"

"You can buy another main course if you want," Lisa told him.

The guy pointed at me. "How come he doesn't have to?"

"Are *you* homeless?" Lisa asked.

It was one of those moments when everything stops. I knew Lisa didn't intend anything mean by what she'd said, but it didn't matter. The guy scowled at me and I felt my face go hot and red.

And it didn't end there. When I got to the lunch table where the usual suspects were huddled in conversation, Tory glanced up and saw me, then whispered something that caused them all to go silent.

Stopping a few feet away from the table, I said, "Sorry. Didn't mean to interrupt. ..."

Talia patted the spot beside her. "Uh ... it's Jen's birthday on Friday, and she wants us all to go Wally's."

Wally's Wowza-Burger was a sort of imitation Planet Hollywood, and it wasn't cheap. Talia said, "We can go, right?" and gave me a look that I interpreted as, *Don't worry, I'll pay for everything.*

6 **lackadaisical** lazy – 11 **tater tot** dish made from deep-fried potatoes – 18 **scowled** made a facial expression of dislike and anger – 20 **huddled** close together, in a tight group – 27 **Planet Hollywood** chain of theme restaurants inspired by Hollywood

Unfortunately, I was pretty sure that everyone else at the table read that look as well. For the second time in less than two minutes, I felt my face go red with embarrassment.

Congratulations, Dan, you're now an official charity case. And everyone knows it.

***

They say timing is everything, but what they don't add is that it's true of bad timing as well. They also say that things come in threes. After being publicly humiliated twice in less time than it takes to lace up a pair of cleats, I couldn't wait for lunch to end. Food wasn't the only thing simmering in the cafeteria at that point. So was I. As soon as Talia and I left, I planned to ask her to be a little less obvious about the signals she sent in front of her friends.

"Yo, Dan." Out in the hall the scraggly haired kid came around the sign-up table and planted himself in front of me, blocking my path, intruding in my space. Then he said, "I mean, come on."

That may have been what he said, but it wasn't what I heard. What I heard was, Dude, now that *the whole school* knows you're living in Dignityville, how can you *not* sign up for the march?

I snapped. Grabbed his collar and yanked him toward me until our faces were so close that I could count the blackheads dotting his nose and forehead.

"Hey!" he cried, clamping his hands around my wrists and struggling to get out of my grip; but the only things clenched more tightly than my fistful of shirt collar were my teeth.

Everyone in the hall stopped and stared.

"Dan!" Talia gasped.

"Jeez, man, come on!" The kid squirmed.

It was over in a flash. I'd made a mistake, and let go.

10 **to lace up** to tighten – 10 **cleats** shoes made stronger with a piece of metal and used for sports

Red-faced and breathing hard, the scraggly haired kid scuttled back around the table. Feeling everyone's eyes, I raised my hands, palms out. "No harm, no foul." It must have sounded lame, but it was all that I could think of.

Talia tugged my arm and we started down the hall again. "What was *that* about?" she hissed, as if *she* was the one who'd been embarrassed.

"Maybe my girlfriend freaking out because I'm temporarily homeless?" I spat angrily.

"I'm not the one who's freaking out. I just ... wish it didn't have to be this way."

"And you think I don't?" I asked incredulously.

She had chemistry next and we stopped outside the lab, but neither of us spoke. Finally, Talia let out a long, dramatic sigh. "Let's just go to Wally's on Friday and have a good time, okay?"

"Sure," I mumbled. "Whatever."

8 **freaking out** *(inf)* getting upset and behaving irrationally

19

That night on the phone Talia and I smoothed things over. But it was starting to feel like each time we saw each other, a problem developed that related to me being homeless. And this time there were other repercussions. The next morning after second period, Noah and I were passing the counseling office when Ms. Reuben came out. "Oh, Dan," she said as if seeing me reminded her of something. "Don't go anywhere." She went back into her office and returned with a folder. "You've got a study hall seventh period. Why don't you come down here."

"How come?"

"We'll chat about your current situation."

Had this happened to Meg, too? For the next few periods I kept an eye out for her. Maybe she could give me an idea of what I was in for. But seventh period arrived before she did.

When I got to the counseling office, Ms. Reuben wasn't alone. Coach Buder and Mrs. Collins, the school psychologist, were also there. "Have a seat, Dan," Ms. Reuben said cheerfully.

What's Buddha doing here? I wondered.

Ms. Reuben interlaced her fingers and leaned forward with a smile. She was a hefty lady with rosy cheeks. "So, how are you?" she asked, like this was just some friendly get-together.

"Fine, thanks."

She nodded as if that was what she'd expected me to say.

"And your family?" asked Mrs. Collins, looking concerned through her large, round glasses.

"They're fine. We're all fine. Look, whatever's going on is just temporary, okay? It's not like I'm the only kid in school who … who doesn't have a place to live right now."

"We understand," Ms. Reuben said with a phony smile. "We just want to make sure you're okay. Are you getting enough to eat?"

4 **repercussions** *(pl)* consequences – 5 **counseling office** a school counselor assists you in your school career – 20 **hefty** big and heavy

"Yes." *Even if I was accepting handouts from the lunch ladies.*

"Did you know you probably qualify for the free breakfast and lunch program here at school?" added Mrs. Collins.

The bus circle was right outside the cafeteria, so every morning the free breakfast kids were on display for everyone who took a bus. I couldn't imagine myself being part of that spectacle.

On the other hand, free lunch sounded great as long as some gong didn't ring every time I got one. "I wouldn't mind free lunch, thanks."

"Excellent." Mrs. Collins wrote something down on a pad. You could see it made her feel good to be able to help. "Do you need an address?"

"Sorry?"

"For your mail. We can arrange for you to get it here."

"Oh, uh, thanks, but my dad got us a post office box."

"Do you take the school bus, Dan?" Ms. Reuben asked.

"Not if I can avoid it."

"We recently arranged for a stop ... so that it's not immediately obvious where you're living? It was a bit tricky because officially, you no longer live in the school district."

"But of course you can stay and finish the year," Mrs. Collins added hastily.

That was a jolt. It had never occurred to me that if you had to move because you were homeless, you might have to change schools, too.

"We'd also like you to get a free yearbook," said Ms. Reuben as if I'd just won a prize on some game show. "You won't have to pay for a ticket to the winter formal and we can give you an extra locker."

Huh? "So I'll have a place to stay at night?"

Buddha grunted like he was trying to suppress a laugh. Mrs. Collins shot him a dirty look, then said, "Some students find they need space for extra things."

That made me wonder. "How many of us are there?"

Mrs. Collins and Ms. Reuben shared a quick glance.

"Let's focus on you," said Mrs. Collins.

"Is it a secret?" I asked.

"It's a sensitive issue."

"In other words, more than people think?"

"So ... we heard there was an incident at lunch yesterday?" Mrs. Collins changed the subject.

I knew that would come up. "Yeah, my bad. Kind of lost it. One of those perfect storm things, you know? I mean, the kid's okay, right? All I did was grab his shirt."

From the silence that followed, I could tell that my response had caught them off guard. Finally Mrs. Collins crossed her legs and leaned forward with an earnest expression. "Dan, giving a glib acknowledgment of what happened doesn't necessarily mean you've accepted the pathology behind it."

Excuse me?

"None of us can remember you doing anything like that before," added Ms. Reuben.

"Yeah, well, I was never homeless before."

The slightest smile appeared on Buddha's lips, but he quickly crushed it.

"So you acknowledge your current situation had something to do with it?" Mrs. Collins asked.

"I sure hope so," I said.

The school psychologist's forehead wrinkled. "You *hope* so?"

"I'd hate to think I'd do something like that for no reason."

Buddha smiled again and both women gave him a murderous look.

"Dan, the purpose of being here isn't to demonstrate how skilled you are at finessing your way out of what happened," Ms. Reuben said. "Things like that occur for a reason. And we're concerned."

I took a deep breath and let it out slowly. "Okay, seriously? Being in my situation sucks. I'm not gonna pretend it doesn't. But I think so far I've handled it pretty well. Yeah, yesterday

6 **my bad** *(sl)* my fault – 12 **glib** superficial – 28 **to finess** *(AE)* to maneuver

I blew it. But here's what I'm thinking. Maybe instead of putting me under a microscope for every little mistake … instead you could cut me some slack? I know what I did was wrong, but I caught myself, right? Did it ever occur to you to put a positive spin on this? Like, 'Hey, Dan, we're proud of how you handled the situation yesterday. Someone else might have let it get out of control, but you really nipped it in the bud. Way to go, dude.'"

Buddha smiled *and* nodded with approval, which constituted about the biggest display of emotion on his part that I could ever recall. Both Ms. Reuben and Mrs. Collins gave him cold glares.

"We just want to make sure there isn't something more we can do to help," said Mrs. Collins.

"Hey, I'll take the free lunch and the extra locker, but unless you can find my parents jobs and a place to live, what else is there?"

"What we *can* do is be here for you," Ms. Reuben said. "We want you to feel like you can come to us with any concern or problem, okay?"

"Uh, sure, thanks."

Mrs. Collins checked her watch. "I guess that's all."

As we got up, out of the corner of my eye I saw Mrs. Collins exchange a look with Buddha, as if it was now his turn to step up. He and I left the office together and went out into the hall.

"They brought you in to be the closer?" I asked.

Coach Buder shrugged. "Moral support."

"Seriously, coach, I'm coping. What else is there to say?"

I'd meant the question to be rhetorical, but Buddha paused and gazed out the windows. It was windy, and bright swarms of orange, yellow, and red leaves swirled past. "You know how they

1 **I blew it** I lost my temper – 3 **to cut sb some slack** *(idm)* to tolerate sb's wrong behavior once – 5 **spin** *(inf)* view – 7 **to nip sth in the bud** *(idm)* to stop sth before it develops further – 7 **way to go** well done – 7 **dude** guy – 25 **closer** relief pitcher *(Unterstützer)*

say playing outfield is the loneliest position in baseball?" he asked. "Well, I think it's pitcher. When you're on the mound, it's all on your shoulders."

Coach Buder glanced back down the hall at the counseling office. "What you have to do on the field is difficult enough, Dan. Don't make it hard for yourself off the field too. If you need help, ask for it, okay? You don't have to do it all alone, and you shouldn't try."

2 **mound** small hill the pitcher stands on

20

A PHONE CALL

"Have you decided?"

"I'd like to know what you're planning."

"That's not your concern."

"Exactly what do I get if I help you?"

"A place to live."

"What kind of place?"

"A house, with enough of a yard for a nice garden."

"In the school district?"

"Yes. So, are you going to help me, or not?"

"If I do, how do I know you'll keep your half of the bargain?"

"I'll have no choice. You'll know something about me that I won't want anyone else to know."

"I see ... all right. I think I can put you in touch with the kind of person you're looking for."

10 **bargain** agreement

21

Whap! The pistol-shot smack of the catcher's mitt reverberated through the air when Noah caught the pitch I'd just thrown. In my mind my conversation with Buddha the day before was more motivation to begin pitching again.

But while things felt good on the pitching mound, they didn't feel so great back "home." It was the Friday of our second week in Dignityville and Mom had started working on the new garden, planting fall vegetables like cabbage, carrots, and beets. Later that evening in the dim light of the dining tent you could see that her face was rosy and glowing after a day of physical labor. But beside her Dad looked pale and grim as he told us the Subaru's transmission was shot and we didn't have the money to repair it.

"The guy at the junkyard will give me a couple hundred bucks for it," he said.

We'd lost our house. Now we were losing our car. A couple hundred bucks wouldn't last long. It was starting to feel like we'd be stuck in Dignityville forever. With Talia's voice echoing in my ears, I asked if he'd come across any job possibilities.

"There's nothing out there," he said.

But there has to be something, I thought. "You mean, nothing that pays better than unemployment?"

Dad and Mom exchanged a furtive look, then Dad said, "Unemployment ran out."

That's how I learned we were applying for food stamps and something called TANF–Temporary Assistance for Needy Families–which was basically just another name for welfare. My parents said they would use the food stamps for their breakfasts and lunches, but I wished we could have used them that night,

1 **to reverberate** to echo strongly – 12 **transmission** mechanism that transmits power from a car's engine to the driving wheels – 12 **shot** *(inf)* ruined – 22 **unemployment** *(inf)* unemployment benefits (money from the state) – 27 **welfare** financial help given to people in need by the government

because someone got the Dignityville menu mixed up and the result was hot dogs, creamed spinach, and beets.

"Remind me not to be homeless in my next lifetime," our neighbor Fred grumbled good-naturedly when he and his wife, Diane, joined us in the dining tent.

"Now, now, Fred," Diane teased. "You're the one who's always saying beggars can't be choosers."

"Maybe, but you never heard me say it when I was hungry."

Meg sat down with us and had started to eat when Joel came by.

"Know where Aubrey is?" he asked.

"He's working tonight."

Joel made a face. "I was hoping he could help me with the bikes."

"I'll help you," Meg said. "Just let me finish dinner."

"You're a good little sister, " Diane said after Joel left.

"I've been well trained," Meg replied, and then told us stories about what it was like having Aubrey for a big brother. Like how, when she was eight, she had to be a vegan because *he* was going through *his* vegan period, and when she was eleven he made her feel so guilty about her favorite leather cowboy boots that she'd stopped wearing them, and everything else that came from animals.

Meg could be pretty funny when she felt like it, and everyone except Dad laughed. At the end of dinner she asked me if I wanted to join her helping Joel, but I was on cleanup detail again and after that Talia and I were supposed to go to Jen's birthday party at Wally's Wowza-Burger. Gradually the others left the table. Fred and Diane headed back to their tent and Mom went to babysit Stella so that Mona could go to work. Soon it was just me and Dad, who sat with his head in his hands, looking morose.

"You okay?" I asked, concerned.

7 **beggars can't be choosers** *(idm)* those in need must accept what they get – 26 **detail** *(AE)* work duty organized by a group – 31 **morose** [mə'rəʊs] melancholy and miserable

He looked up. Maybe it was the dim light, but his eyes looked deep and hollow."Oh, yeah, for a total failure I'm great."

That caught me by surprise. He'd never sounded so utterly defeated before.

"No," I said. "You've been a damn good father."

"And look where we've wound up." He gestured around the dining tent.

"It's not you, it's the economy."

Dad shook his head slowly. "I let this happen. I know Mom says she's happy, but she just wants to see the good side of everything."

"Don't beat yourself up. We'll figure something out."

Dad stared at the table and didn't reply.

"Listen," I said. "If you're a failure, so is every parent who ever stayed home to raise their kids. And how can you say you're a failure? What about all those inner-city kids you kept from joining gangs?"

"The program's gone. What do you think those kids are doing now?" He hung his head. Seeing him so depressed made me feel guilty that I'd ever gotten angry at him for allowing us to wind up here. Not everyone was born to be a great businessman. In his own way he'd done the best he could, and no matter what he said now, he probably *had* made a difference for a lot of those disadvantaged kids.

And there was something else. "Hey, I wouldn't be going to Rice next year if it wasn't for you."

Dad looked up and the corners of his mouth rose with pride. "Yeah." But the smile was brief and was soon replaced by a faraway look. "I ever tell you that senior year of high school was probably the best time I ever had? From the second I got accepted on early admission it was one big party." His lips firmed. "Meanwhile *you* get to spend senior year in a tent. ... You deserve better, Dan. You really do."

12 **to beat os up** to reproach/blame os – 24 **disadvantaged** poor, underprivileged

I'm not sure I'd ever seen Dad so down. Even though I was supposed to be cleaning up the dining room, I sat there with him, afraid to let him be alone. Outside, people were still coming home from work. I couldn't get used to the idea that you could have a full-time job and still be homeless, but the evidence was all around us. Of course, there were the others–disheveled, with tattered clothes, missing teeth, unshaven and unsteady, the ones you suspected weren't exactly following the Dignityville rules about sobriety.

I'd once looked down on people like that. To be honest, I'd felt superior. But not anymore.

Dad rose up from his seat. "You better get to work."

"Sure you'll be okay?" I asked.

He smiled weakly. "Don't worry about me."

As I started across the dining tent, I glanced at the TV in the back. Now that dinner was over, the usual crowd had gathered for the evening's entertainment. The local news was on and they were reporting that the police had just discovered a beating victim behind Ruby's Bar and Grill. He'd been identified as the restaurant's bartender.

6 **disheveled** [dɪˈʃevᵊld] untidy

PART TWO

22

It's pouring outside the emergency room. Meg and I stand under the canopy, chilled by the cold mist as rain roars down. Dignityville is nearly three miles away, and we'll get soaked if we try to walk. There's a cab at the curb … if only I had money for the fare.

Meg digs into her pocket and I feel like crap. Her brother's been nearly beaten to death and now *she's* got to pay for the ride home?

She counts what she pulls out of her pocket. "I've got enough." We run out into the rain.

The cabby needs to know where we're going.

"Know Dignityville?" I ask.

"Who doesn't?" he answers. I expect him to start driving, but he looks over the seat at me. "Sure you got the fare?"

"Yeah."

In the back of the cab I put my arm around Meg and she sniffs miserably. Could things be any worse? If I've read between the lines correctly, her brother may not even make it through the night. Back "home" in Dignityville her father's deathly ill. I wish I knew what to say, but anything that comes to mind feels like some movie cliché.

There, there, everything's going to be okay.

Yeah, right.

"I can't stop thinking about them hitting him with a baseball bat," she sniffs.

The cabdriver looks at us in the rearview mirror. "That beating tonight?"

"You know about it?" I ask, surprised.

He holds up something that looks like a walkie-talkie. "Police scanner. He gonna be okay?"

1 **emergency room** section in a hospital where victims with sudden and serious medical problems are treated *(Notaufnahme)*

Our eyes meet in the rearview mirror and I shake my head, not because I know what's going to happen to Aubrey, but because this isn't the time to talk about it. He nods back.

Ten minutes later we stop in front of Dignityville. When Meg tries to pay, the driver shakes his head. "Forget it. I was heading in this direction anyway."

We thank him multiple times and then run down the muddy path in the dark, the rain making *pocking* sounds on the cloth roofs of the tents. When we get to Meg's she turns to me, her hair plastered to her head and rainwater dripping down her face. "Thank you, Dan. I ... I don't know what I would have done ..." She seems so frail and wounded, and the next thing I know, even though we're standing in the rain getting drenched, I take her in my arms and hug her.

Jogging back to my tent through the rain, my feet are soaked and squishy in my shoes. Here and there in the dark bikes are propped against the fence or leaning against tent posts–the results of Aubrey's bike drive. My phone vibrates again. Talia. That makes seven messages from her, and I've got that dismal feeling like when I've thrown a bad game and in the locker room the reporters from the local newspaper and radio station are going to ask what happened. As if I ever know how to answer.

Gee, guys, guess I just didn't have my good stuff today.

According to my horoscope, Venus in Capricorn forms a square to Saturn in Libra, which tends to make my curveball hang.

Our tent is empty. Inside I pull off my soaked jacket and shoes, dry my head with a towel, pull on a fresh hoodie and dry socks.

Then, as much as I dread it, I call Talia back. "Hey."

"Where are you?" She sounds hurt. "Why haven't you answered my texts?"

10 **plastered to** stuck on – 12 **frail** [freɪl] weak – 16 **squishy** making a gurgling sound – 19 **dismal** awful and sad – 25 **curveball** a ball pitched in a curving path (to make it more difficult to hit) – 28 **to dread** [dred] to be afraid of

I make up a lie about how I was waiting at the Gerson Street bus stop when Meg passed on her way to the hospital and told me about what had happened to Aubrey. And how I could tell she needed support and I went with her.

"Aubrey?"

"Her brother. The one who's kind of the leader of Dignityville."

"Is Meg there?" is all Talia wants to know.

"She's in her tent. But think about it, Tal. The guys who beat up Aubrey couldn't have known he lived in Dignityville unless someone told them. It really sounds like they beat him up on purpose."

As if she hasn't heard a word I've said, she says, "Can you still come to the party?"

It's almost eleven and I'm toast, but that never stopped me from going out before. Sooner or later you catch a second wind. That's not what's holding me back. It's just hard to imagine partying after what happened to Aubrey. "Better not, sorry."

Silence on the other end of the line. Then Talia says, "I have to go," and hangs up.

She's never done that before.

The patter of rain against the tent is slowing, and I wonder where my parents are. It's not like they can afford to go out. Not wanting to be alone, I go over to the dining tent. Mom's sitting by herself, reading a book. She gives me a puzzled look when I sit down. "Aren't you supposed to be out with Talia?"

I tell her about Aubrey.

"Oh, God." She puts down the book. "That's awful."

"Dad around?" I ask.

"I think he's refereeing a softball game."

They play softball under the lights on Friday nights, but … "Mom, it's been pouring."

14 **I'm toast** *(sl)* I'm really tired – 15 **to catch a second wind** [wɪnd] *(inf)* to find new energy after feeling tired – 29 **softball** a slower and less dangerous version of baseball

She blinks with slow surprise as if she hadn't put together the weather and Dad's plans. "Basketball?"

"I don't think the season's started yet. And it's eleven at night."

She shrugs. "Well, whatever."

Because of the damp chill inside the Grand Ballroom, they've turned on the heaters. The radiated warmth provides a tiny bit of comfort in an otherwise seriously uncomfortable situation. I've managed to reach seventeen years old without ever knowing anyone around my age who's died. Not that I didn't think it could happen, but until it becomes a real possibility for someone you know, I'm not sure you truly believe it.

As if she's read my mind, Mom presses her lips together sympathetically. "People recover from comas all the time."

We talk about Meg and what it must be like for her and her mother with Mr. Fine already sick and Aubrey now in the hospital. Just when I feel like I've gotten out most of what's on my mind, I realize there's still one more thing: "Talia's mad because I didn't go to the party. But after what happened to Aubrey, how could anyone feel like partying?"

"Do you know what that's called?" Mom asks.

There's a *name* for it? "Partyitis?"

"Social conscience. The injustices of life bother you."

I raise my hands in a gesture of wonder. Like, what did I do to get stuck with a social conscience?

"I know," Mom agrees. "It's not always fun, but it's good. The world could use more of it."

Her comment makes me think back to the night my friends and I made chili in the basement at Saint Stephen's, and how Tory and Ben, two of my least favorite people, were the ones who showed the most concern for the folks in Dignityville. I think of how Mom is trying to get some of the residents of Dignityville involved in gardening instead of spending all day watching TV, and I tell her I'm proud of what she's doing.

She nods, but not with great enthusiasm. "Now, if only you and your father were happier."

"Why doesn't Dad take a job? I mean, any job? Even pumping gas?"

"I think he's depressed, sweetheart. It's hard for him to find the motivation."

He's given up.

23

A phone vibrating somewhere in the tent wakes us the next morning. Mom and I search through our things until she finds it and squints. "'C U in 5?'"

"It's Noah," I groan. "Sorry."

I drag my butt out of my sleeping bag and start to pull on some running clothes. Dad came back late last night, but now his sleeping bag is empty, which means he must've gotten up early and left. *What's he up to?*

I trudge toward the entrance where Noah's waiting, and we start to jog. The rains have mostly passed, but the sky is still overcast and the ground is wet, so we stick to sidewalks. "What happened last night? Tory said Talia was really upset."

I tell him about Aubrey.

"Holy crap," he mutters. "But wait, how would beating up one guy change anything about Dignityville?"

I tell him how–despite what Mayor George said about Dignityville being temporary–Aubrey was working toward making it permanent. "A lot of people are convinced the value of their homes will go down if the town is crawling with homeless people. It's all about money."

"So you kill the beast by cutting off its head," Noah says.

"Exactly."

"Shouldn't be that hard to figure out who's behind it," he adds, almost offhandedly.

As we continue to jog, I stare at him, dumbfounded."How?"

"It's a seriously desperate act, right?" he replies as if the answer is obvious. "Something only someone who had an awful lot to lose would even consider. So you start with those who have the most to lose."

He's right. It's a shockingly simple deduction. Except there could still be so many possible suspects–including those I don't

3 **squints** looks with her eyes partly closed – 14 **Holy crap** *(inf) Ach du Scheiße!* – 19 **crawling with** very full of – 25 **dumbfounded** silent with astonishment

know and may have never heard of–that trying to figure it out feels futile.

We jog through town. A light drizzle begins to filter out of the clouds, but it doesn't bother us. My thoughts drift back to Talia. What if, by tonight, she and I still haven't spoken? The idea of spending another Saturday night hanging around Dignityville is seriously less than appealing.

I ask Noah if he's got plans.

He shoots me a look out of the corner of his eye. "Tyler, Zach, and I are going to see Narconna."

That catches me by surprise. He knows they're one of my favorite bands.

"The tickets are, like, pretty expensive," he adds.

Ouch! How sucky is this?

"Yeah, I probably couldn't have gone anyway," I agree, trying to smooth it over.

It's time to head back to Dignityville, and we talk about the World Series for the rest of the way. Neither Noah nor I care much for either team, but at least it's something safe to discuss. At a stoplight I look to my right. About a block away a guy with a big plastic bag is going through garbage cans. He's wearing a hat and sunglasses, which is strange because it's overcast and misty, and besides, when was the last time you saw a bum wearing sungla–

Wait a minute. ... There's something disturbingly familiar ... Is that ... No ... no way ...

I turn away before Noah notices what I'm looking at. The light changes. We start to jog again. Inside, my stomach twists and churns.

Couldn't it be someone who just looks like him?
With those sunglasses you can't really be sure, right?
Things can't be THAT *bad, can they?*

14 **sucky** *(AE sl)* unpleasant – 18 **World Series** championship series of US pro baseball games

A block later I realize my hands are clenched so tight the fingernails are digging into my palms.

Face it, Dan. It was Dad.

At the entrance to Dignityville I tell Noah to have fun at the concert and we say good-bye. I'm still in shock over what I just saw. Why *shouldn't* things be that bad? Dad's unemployment has run out. He mentioned food stamps and TANF.

Should I tell Mom what he's been up to? Or let Dad know I know? I need to think about this. Meanwhile, stepping back into Dignityville is such a weird, jarring experience, like passing through a Stargate wormhole and coming out in some Third World refugee camp where people live in tents and the sidewalks are muddy.

It really is *The Grapes of Wrath* all over again.

7 **TANF** *abb for:* "Temporary Assistance for Needy Families", a federal program which helps families in need to achieve self-sufficiency – 10 **jarring** annoying, irritating – 11 **Stargate** science-fiction film and TV series; also the name of a fictional device allowing people to be transported to a faraway destination – 11 **wormhole** a fictional tunnel said to connect different parts of the universe

24

The Fines live in a tan army surplus tent with plastic roll-up windows. I stop outside for a moment, uncertain how to proceed. Tents don't have doorbells, and I don't want to track mud in. Finally I go to the front flap and clear my throat. "Uh, excuse me?"

"Dan?" Meg's voice darts out from inside. "Just a minute."

When the flap opens I catch a glimpse of a hospital bed. Just like that old lady in the ER last night, Meg's dad has a greenish breathing mask over his face. He's pale and bony with a smattering of uncombed white hair, and looks like he's asleep.

Meg quickly closes the flap behind her, then gestures to me to walk. "We don't want him to know," she whispers. "He thinks Aubrey has a job out of town."

"How is he?"

"He made it through the night." As she walks, Meg hugs herself like she's trying to hold it together. "The doctor said if he continues to improve they could move him out of the ICU in a day or two."

"Great!"

She nods halfheartedly.

Thinking back to my conversation with Noah, I ask, "Has anyone been able to talk to him about what happened?"

Meg shakes her head. "He's still in a coma."

We walk around to the back of the park, where Mom and about half a dozen others are turning over soil with shovels and rakes. She sees us, smiles, and waves. Still picturing Dad and his big plastic bag, I force a smile and wave back. Does she know what he's been doing? I bet she doesn't.

A tree-lined stream runs through the back of the park, and Meg and I head that way. We settle down on some rocks beside the bank. "And your dad?" I ask.

1 **tan** brownish – 1 **surplus tent** extra-large, stable tent – 4 **flap** piece of cloth (i.e. the door here) – 10 **smattering** small amount

Meg shrugs. “The same. There’s nothing anyone can do. We’re just waiting for him, too.”

Only he’s headed in the opposite direction.

“Isn’t there someplace he can go?” I ask. “What do they call those places?”

“A hospice? He’s not ready. They don’t want you until … the end.” Her voice cracks. I put my arm around her and she leans close. Dead leaves drift past on the muddy water.

“I keep thinking about *The Grapes of Wrath*,” I tell her. “And we’re the Okies.”

“What about your scholarship?”

“I could get hurt, or just not be good enough.”

“Don’t say that.”

I brush some curls away from her face. “And what about you?”

“I don’t know,” she says. “Aubrey took out all those college loans to get a degree in political science and the only job he could find was bartending. And he still has to pay the loans back. You really have to wonder if college is worth it. I mean, if I graduate with tons of loans and can’t get a decent job? I could be in debt for years. Might be better off getting a job right after high school.”

I don’t say what I’m thinking: *Sure, you could get some crap job after high school, but if you don’t go to college you’ll be stuck in crap jobs for the rest of your life.*

But these days even some people who go to college get stuck in crap jobs.

Or no jobs at all.

I don’t say it … because I’m pretty sure I don’t have to. Meg already knows. Meanwhile, other thoughts plague me. I wish Noah hadn’t made that connection to who would have wanted Aubrey out of the picture. I wish I knew what to do about Dad. Could I sell my laptop? Bad idea. It’s four years old and probably

10 **Okies** *(off, sl)* poor migrant farm workers who left Oklahoma during the Great Depression of the 1930s – 15 **college loan** money you borrow to pay for your education and pay back over time – 22 **crap** *(inf)* bad, useless

not worth the price of a good family meal. And then what would I do for homework and college next year?

I wish there were something I could do for Meg. I'm getting tired of wondering how this happened to us. I'm getting tired of wondering what's wrong with this country. Right now I just wish I could find a way to make things better.

25

A PHONE CALL

"Did you hear what happened to that kid? Is that what you were planning all along? Is that why you wouldn't tell me what you were going to do? Are you out of your–"

"Calm down. It was a mistake. Things got out of hand."

"Out of hand? He's in a coma, for God's sake!"

"I said calm down. Listen to me. It wasn't supposed to happen like that. They were just supposed to scare him. Get him to stop."

"Try telling *that* to his parents."

"Enough. It's terrible, but there's nothing we can do about it now. Maybe things may have gotten a bit more complicated, but we can still make it work to our advantage."

"'We'? Are you insane? I won't have anything more to do with this."

"Oh, I think you will … unless you want your son to find out."

26

On Sunday Uncle Ron picks us up and takes us back to his house for dinner. For the first time in weeks we all have a meal together. The twins seem really happy to see me, and everyone is on their best behavior.

Later, Ron drives us back to Dignityville. It's silent in the car, as if no one can think of a safe topic to discuss. Not Ron's business, not being homeless, not Mom's garden …

We stop outside Dignityville and start to get out of the car. As I slide across the seat toward the door, Ron extends his clenched hand toward me. He waits until my parents' backs are turned and then opens his hand. A bunch of $20 bills tumble out. I'll give them to Mom later.

At school on Monday when I come out of the kitchen with my free lunch, Talia's nestled cozily at the table, surrounded by a bunch of her girlfriends. Over the weekend I texted and called a few times and always got her voice mail. So I backed off and gave her time to cool down. Obviously she's still not ready to talk.

There are plenty of other places to sit. As I wander through the cafeteria with my tray, various people wave. But rather than join them, I pick a table by myself and start to eat. I guess I just don't want to risk getting into an awkward conversation about what's going on in my life right now.

But then the scraggly haired kid passes carrying a tray. Now it's my turn to call to him. "Yo."

He stops, frowns.

I clear my throat. "I owe you an apology."

He cocks his head uncertainly. "Sure, thanks." Starts to turn away.

14 **nestled cozily** *here* sitting in a comfortable and relaxed position

"No, seriously, have a seat."

"Why?"

"Let's talk." I pat the tabletop. "Come on."

Looking doubtful, he sits.

"What's your name?" I ask.

"Mason."

"Sophomore?"

"Junior."

"So here's the thing," I tell him. "I totally blew it the other day."

He nods slowly.

"But I'm curious," I go on. "Why me? You think that if I sign up, the other jocks will want to go too? And then all the cheerleaders?"

He leans back and gives me a puzzled look. "How can you joke about it? I mean, given your situation, don't you want to do something?"

Why does it still feel like a punch in the gut every time someone points out that I'm homeless? Like I still can't accept it. "Sorry, man, protest marches aren't my thing."

Mason leans forward. "They're *everybody's* thing. You know that nearly one-third of this country is living at or near the poverty level? That's one out of every three people. More than a hundred million are either poor or close to it."

"Not around here."

"No, but ten miles down the road in Burlington they sure are," Mason says. "If we don't fix what's wrong, this country's screwed. Only nothing serious is being done because the politicians and rich people who fund their election campaigns aren't the ones who are suffering. I'm not saying they don't care, but maybe they don't care *enough*. To them poverty is just another political football to kick around. Like global warming and health care and instability in the Middle East. That's why we have to get

17 **gut** stomach – 26 **to be screwed** *(sl)* be in serious trouble

their attention. Believe me, Dan, when they see a million people jamming the streets of Washington demanding change, they're gonna notice."

Can't argue with that. "Okay, this won't sound important to you, but there's a baseball tournament Thanksgiving weekend."

Mason sits back with a disappointed frown. "What if you miss it?"

"Pro scouts come. It's a chance to get seen."

"You think they don't already know who you are? How many high school pitchers have an eighty-eight-mile-an-hour fastball and a nasty curve?"

I stare at him. Knowing he caught me off guard, Mason smiles. "You didn't think I could be political *and* a baseball fan?"

I smile back, but mostly because I'm not sure what else to do.

He starts to get up. "I have to get to the table. I'm the only one out there these days." He picks up his tray, then pauses and drops his voice. "So seriously, what's it like at Dignityville?"

"Sucks."

He thinks for a moment. "Listen, if things get bad? I mean, really bad? Let's talk, okay? I think my parents might be able to help."

He leaves. That's the kid I grabbed by the collar and came about an inch from beating into a pulp.

Think about it.

We're not *really* poor. Even if we're homeless and have no jobs or money.

It's just temporary.

Things will get better.

Not that I know how.

Mom seems happy as long as she has a garden, but it won't make her a penny.

11 **nasty** *here:* aggressive and difficult to play – 23 **pulp** shapeless mass

Dad's miserable.

And I have a full ride to Rice. As long as I pitch well and keep my grades up, that should get me through college. But what will I do over vacations? Will I be able to afford to come home? And if I do, will I have to stay in a tent with my parents?

Meg isn't in school today. Did she skip because of Aubrey? Has something bad happened? If I had one of our cell phones I'd text her.

School's ending and Talia and I still haven't spoken. We've never gone this long without talking before. Maybe she's waiting for me to apologize, or just show that I care.

I look for her at her locker, but she isn't there.

As I go around the corner I imagine her waiting at my locker.

No such luck. Okay, guess I can go over to her house later and attempt some kind of grand romantic gesture. Stand on her lawn under her bedroom window holding up a boom box playing some seriously syrupy love song. If that won't win her back, nothing will.

Noah's expecting me in the gym, along with Tyler and Zach, who want to take batting practice, but all I can think about is Talia, and my parents, and who might be behind Aubrey's beating.

This is a problem. You can't throw with garbage in your mind. It gets in the way. You've got to have that clear, well-lit tunnel straight from your arm to the catcher's mitt. Somehow I know that throwing today is going to be a bust. I won't be focused. I'll be wasting my and Noah's time.

I turn around and do something I never thought I'd do.

Head for the bus circle.

After asking a monitor which one to take, I board a bus and that old smell hits me–gym socks, vinyl seats, and diesel exhaust. It's

2 **a full ride** *(inf)* a scholarship that pays a student's entire college costs – 26 **bust** *(AE, sl)* failure

like going back in time. I half expect to see eleven-year-old versions of my friends waving and patting empty spots for me to sit. Instead it's a sea of kids' faces staring because they've never seen me on the bus before.

I take a seat near the front, next to a girl who looks like she's in seventh grade. Immediately, she presses herself into the corner and looks back at the two girls in the seat behind her, who giggle, probably because they're her friends and they're completely amused that this senior is sitting next to her.

Even the bus driver's looking at me in the rearview mirror like she doesn't know what I'm doing there.

The bus can't go until the five in front of it move, and there's some kind of delay, so we sit. The girl next to me keeps glancing back at her friends, who keep tittering. She's wearing a necklace with the name STACI spelled out in silver letters, and I'm starting to wonder if this is a mistake and whether I should get off and walk home … and that's when someone raps on the window.

It's Noah.

I get up, lean over Staci, and slide the window down. Noah's got a *WTF?* look on his face.

"I gotta go home," I tell him. Meanwhile, poor Staci's cowering in the corner of our seat and the two girls behind her are practically gagging in near hysteria.

"You were just gonna leave me there?" Noah asks with a frown.

"I figured you could practice with Zach and Tyler. Zach can throw."

Noah turns his palms upward. "What the hell?"

"Seriously, I gotta go," I repeat. "We'll work out tomorrow, I promise."

He gives me an annoyed, frustrated look, and then the bus driver says I have to sit because we're leaving. I take my seat. Staci and her friends have gone silent, like they're breathlessly waiting to see what happens next. So I put my arm around Staci's

20 **WTF?** *(sl, abb)* what the fuck?

shoulders and turn to the two behind us. “I don’t know what’s so funny. I love Staci, and someday I’m going to marry her.”

If their eyes got any larger they’d pop out of their sockets. I remove my arm and sit back.

The girls don’t make a sound for the rest of the ride.

A loudly clearing throat wakes me. The bus has stopped and the driver is turned in her seat, giving me the hairy eyeball. I give Staci a peck on the cheek. “Until tomorrow, my love.”

And then get off.

***

There’s a paper cup lying on the dirt path between the tents. I pick it up.

Homeless pride.

Don’t want the place to look like a bunch of bums live here, do we?

Meg’s sitting at one of the tables in the dining tent with her school books. When I join her, she tells me she stayed with her dad today because her mom went to the hospital, where they ran some tests on Aubrey. “He scored a twelve on the Glasgow scale and a five on the Rancho Los Amigos. It’s good news.” If there’s such a thing as a sad smile, she gives it. “It means his brain is still working.”

“What happens next?”

“We see him whenever we can. We talk, play music, make noise. The doctors say it helps. But mostly we wait.”

It’s the middle of the afternoon, and except for the usual crowd around the TV, the dining tent is empty. I’ve stacked my books on the table, but don’t feel like opening them just yet. “I was thinking today what it would be like if my parents wind up here permanently. I mean, like coming back from college and having

14 **bunch of bums** *(AE)* group of homeless tramps – 19 **Glasgow scale** measures the brain activity of a person in a coma – 20 **Rancho Los Amigos** measures the cognitive level in brain-injured patients

to stay in the tent with them. And what happens if my friends want to go out and I don't have any money."

"Don't you go out with Talia now?" Meg asks.

"We …" I hesitate, lie. "Split stuff."

The shame of poverty: I can't admit the truth. In English we're reading *A Streetcar Named Desire,* and I can't help thinking of Blanche DuBois and how at the end she becomes completely delusional. They're taking her to a mental institution and she thinks she's going away with her millionaire boyfriend.

And here I am, living in a tent, qualifying for free school lunches, sponging off my girlfriend, and still pretending I'm *not* poor?

Yo, Blanche, wait up! I'm right there with you!

Just as I feel my spirits really start to sink, Meg closes her hand on mine. "Dan?"

I know she wants me to look at her, but I can't. I glance at the folks at the back watching TV. I gaze outside at the tents and the random junky bikes donated for the bike drive. Maybe I'm going to college next year, but what about my parents? Forget the part about *me* having to come back to Dignityville over vacation, what's *their* life going to be like? Is this it? Is Mom destined to garden and Dad to collect bottles and cans for the rest of their lives?

It doesn't have to be this way. I've read enough *Sports Illustrated* to know that guys who are drafted straight out of high school get million-dollar signing bonuses. I think back to the day Mom said if I really hated it here we'd try something else. *Hey, Dan, did it ever occur to you that maybe it's not up to your parents to get you out of Dignityville? Maybe it's up to* you *to get* them *out?* I start to gather my books.

"You're going?" Meg asks, startled.

4 **split stuff** *(inf, here:)* serious disagreement – 8 **delusional** having false beliefs about os – 11 **to sponge off** *(inf)* to get money etc from a person without doing anything for it

"I, uh, just realized I have to talk to Noah." *A man got to do what he got to do.*

Her eyes widen. I know what she's thinking. I just sat down and already I have to leave?

"Catch you later, okay?" I promise emptily, and head back to my tent. We keep the phones on a small nightstand, and I pick one up and punch Noah's speed dial. I hold the phone to my ear and wait.

It rings once, then a recording comes on telling me that this mobile number is invalid. That's wrong, so I try again … and get the same recording.

I put that phone down and start to reach for the other one when I realize that neither of my parents is here, but both phones are. That never happens, unless … I try the other phone and get the same message–our phone service has been canceled.

It takes a while to find a ride that doesn't have a flat tire. Finally I come across an old mountain bike. The handlebars, gearshift, and chain are brown with rust, but at least the tires are semi-inflated.

At one time it was an eighteen-speed, but now only two gears work, and the chain jumps and skips.

But, hey, beggars can't be choosers.

27

Noah lives in one of the nicer parts of town. By the time I get there, dusk has begun to settle. The outside lights are on and I leave the bike on the lawn, climb the steps to the porch, and ring the bell.

Dr. Williams answers, still wearing his tie from work. He smiles warmly. "Dan, good to see you. Come in."

In the front hall delicious lemon and garlic fragrances waft out of the kitchen and I realize it's just shy of dinnertime and probably not the best moment to drop by.

"Noah!" Dr. Williams calls up the stairs. "Your company's here."

He assumes Noah has invited me over. Noah's younger sister, Deborah, practically bursts out of her bedroom at the top of the stairs. Even though she's in sixth grade, you can see that she's well on her way to being drop-dead gorgeous, with caramel skin, long dark hair, and big eyes. "Hi, Dan!" She waves eagerly. "Here for dinner?"

"Uh …" I don't know how to answer. Whatever they're having smells great, but I have a feeling Noah may not be so eager to have me join them.

"Of course!" Dr. Williams doesn't hesitate. He clamps his hand on my arm and starts to lead me toward the kitchen. "You can have Derek's seat."

In the kitchen Phillipa, the housekeeper, is preparing dinner.

"We'll need another setting, Phillipa," Dr. Williams says. "Dan's joining us."

The kitchen door swings open and Noah comes in with a stony scowl on his face.

"Look who's here," Dr. Williams says.

"Hard to believe," Noah replies, shooting me his second *WTF?* look of the day. "To what do we owe the honor?"

"You didn't–?" Dr. Williams begins, then goes quiet.

7 **garlic fragance** *Knoblauchduft* – 8 **just shy** [ʃaɪ] **of** *here:* shortly before – 14 **drop-dead gorgeous** *(inf)* very attractive

As if to compound the awkwardness, just at that moment Noah's mom, who is also a doctor, comes in and gives me a hug. "So good to see you, Dan."

Is it my imagination or is she being slightly more effusive than normal?

To spare his wife the discomfort that the rest of us are feeling, Noah's dad suggests we sit for dinner. Phillipa serves lemon chicken, roasted potatoes, and string beans. It's the most delicious meal I've had in months. "This is the best, thanks."

Noah's dad smiles weakly. "Noah's told us about your, uh, current situation. I spoke to some of my patients who I thought might be able to help find you part-time work, but they didn't know of anything. But, if there's anything *we* can do ..."

"I really appreciate it, Dr. Williams," I answer.

"It's terrible," adds Noah's mom. "I mean, what's happened to this country?"

"We have no one to blame but ourselves." Noah's dad starts in about companies making more profits by automating their production lines and building factories in China and India, where they pay workers a tenth of what they pay them here. Hence American workers lose their jobs while company owners and shareholders earn more profits. "So the rich get richer and everyone else suffers."

"Uh, no offense or anything, but wouldn't that include you?" I point out.

Noah's parents share a brief look, then his father says, "Not many people would voluntarily choose to be impoverished, Dan. We've been very fortunate, but we've also worked extremely hard."

"You want to get rid of poverty in this country?" Noah grouses. "You can start with the government. If they weren't so bent on helping people *not* find work, it wouldn't be this way."

His mom rolls her eyes and says half-jokingly, "My son, the right-wing conservative."

4 **effusive** enthusiastic, excited – 30 **to grouse** [graʊs] to grumble

After dinner Noah and I go outside. It's dark and the out-door lights are on.

"Sorry about this afternoon." Seems like I've been doing a lot of apologizing lately.

"Sure." He shrugs.

"I mean it. That's why I came over."

"Couldn't wait until tomorrow?"

"Didn't know if I was getting a ride to school in the morning."

Noah smirks. "At least you're honest."

But there's more. "Look, from now on? We're back to workouts six days a week."

Noah nods vacantly, like he's not sure whether to believe me.

"I'm serious. The Fall Classic's my last shot at getting drafted."

His eyes dart curiously at me and I know he's wondering why this sudden change of heart. After I explain how a signing bonus could get my parents out of Dignityville, he glances back at his big, well-lit house. I wonder if we're thinking the same thing: He may have a nice place to live and parents who have good jobs and plenty of money. But otherwise, is he really any different from me? It's just luck. Like we were twins separated at birth and adopted by different families. He holds out his hand. The peace offering. "Okay, white boy, starting tomorrow we kick it up a notch."

"Thanks."

"And one more thing?"

"Yeah?"

"Come back for dinner any time you want."

***

I start to ride through the dark back to Dignityville. The way I look at it, I was on course until we lost our house. Then I got sidetracked. Now it's time to get serious again. The reason I

9 **to smirk** [smɜ:rk] to smile in a self-satisfied or cheeky way – 13 **Fall's Classic** baseball championship – 13 **to be drafted** *(AE) here:* to be selected for a sports team or program (*usu:* for the army) – 15 **signing bonus** sum of money offered to a new player – 23 **to kick up a notch** *(inf)* to increase the physical practice

started pitching was because I've got the arm, the talent, and the head for the position. It's pretty unusual when all three things come together, and that's why I've got the full ride to Rice. That's why Talia and I …

Whoa! I hit the rusty brakes.

Talia …

I'm practically in her neighborhood.

If I really want to get things back on track, that should include her, right?

So here's my moment.

The light's on in Talia's room.

I'd love to do something dramatic and romantic, but short of riding up the walk and crashing onto the porch, nothing comes to mind, so I just climb up the steps and knock.

"Who is it?" a female voice asks from inside.

"Hi, Mrs. Purcellen. It's Dan. Is Talia here?"

"Oh, uh … just a minute, Dan."

Uh-oh … she didn't come to the door to greet me. Not even a, *Why Dan, what a nice surprise!* or *Hi, Dan, how are you?* It's obvious that mother and daughter have been talking.

Talia makes me wait five minutes before the door opens and there she is, back-lit by lights inside, a beautiful silhouette. I instantly feel a yearning that I haven't felt for weeks. I don't want to talk, I just want to pull her close.

Which is exactly what I do.

Later, sitting on the porch, I explain how I got derailed by everything that's happened to my family.

"I should have been more understanding," Talia says.

"No, it's okay. The whole thing kind of came out of left field for both of us."

26 **derailed** off track, distracted – 29 **to come out of left field** *(idm)* to happen very unexpectedly

She puts her arms around me. “I’m glad we’re past it.” We kiss. She holds on tight. “We won’t let anything like this ever happen again, right?”

“Right.” I agree.

“We’ll tell each other when something’s wrong?”

“Yes.”

She leans her head on my shoulder and we sit quietly. I’m relieved that she doesn’t bring up Meg.

A rattling old pickup pulls into the driveway and Talia’s dad gets out wearing a suit and carrying a briefcase. Because of a bad hip, Mr. Purcellen walks with a cane. The pickup’s from back in the days when he first started building houses.

Talia and I slide apart just enough to make it obvious that moments ago we were sitting closer. Mr. Purcellen glances at the bike lying on the curb. “Hello, Dan.”

Talia’s dad can’t be more than five foot eight. The whole family’s small. But what they lack in size they make up with ferocity.

“Hey, Mr. Purcellen.” I jump up and shake his hand.

“That your bike?”

“No, sir, just a communal thing anyone at Dignityville can use.”

Mr. Purcellen purses his lips thoughtfully. “How’s that going for you?”

“It is what it is, sir.”

He turns to his daughter. “Going to be out here long?” It isn’t really a question–more of an order disguised as a question.

“I’ll be in soon, Daddy.”

Her father nods curtly. “Good to see you, Dan. Excuse me while I get some dinner.” He goes inside. It’s after nine o’clock and he’s just gotten home from work.

I drop my voice. “Pretty late for dinner.”

“He’s been putting in long hours.” Talia glances at the door as if to make sure no one’s listening, then whispers, “Business isn’t so good.”

17 **ferocity** aggressiveness

It's hard to know what "isn't so good" means to Talia. The place they rented last summer in Hilton Head was pretty mind blowing. Mr. Purcellen may putter around town in that old pickup, but when he and his wife go out, they take the big Mercedes in the garage.

So, business may not be great, but the Purcellens are about as far away from Dignityville as any family in Median. Truth is, I doubt Talia's ever *seen* the inside of a tent.

But then a thought strikes me–I don't *want* Talia to see the inside of a tent. At least, not *my* tent. I don't want her, or any of my friends, to come to Dignityville. I don't want them to be part of my homeless life because ... well, because I don't want to be part of it either.

We gaze out at an orange harvest moon. Once again I'm struck by how strange it's all become. For most of our lives we've just been kids going to school, fooling around, making friends and being social, living in this protective bubble where whatever's going on in the outside world hasn't had much of an effect on us. But things "out there" change–a company goes out of business or moves its factories to China, a country spends too much money fighting wars and as a result has to cut back on social programs, parents lose jobs, families lose homes, people go broke paying for medical care. The next thing you know, you're still a kid who's supposed to be doing kid stuff, only the protective bubble has burst and now you're living in a tent, never passing a penny without picking it up, and searching for coffee shops with free Wi-Fi so you can do your homework.

At first you think, *This isn't the way it's supposed to be.*

Then you slowly figure out that there's no such thing as "supposed to be" anymore.

There's just the way it is.

3 **to putter around** to move around aimlessly – 17 **protective bubble** mental and physical state that shelters you from harm – 22 **to go broke** to no longer have any money

Talia stretches up for one last kiss, then whispers that she better go inside.

You hate to see the moment end. You don't want to leave this comfortable porch, or let go of this warm, pretty girl. And you realize that it isn't just the comforting softness of the girl beside you, but that for a few precious moments you were back inside the protective bubble.

And now you have to get on that rusty bike and ride back to Dignityville.

28

For the rest of the week Noah and I work on my pitching. Aubrey is still in a coma, and even though the doctors say his scores are improving, there's no way to know for certain if he'll ever wake up. I see Meg at school and at Dignityville and we talk about her brother, but don't really spend time together. She sees me at lunch and in the hall with Talia, so she must get the picture. I feel kind of bad about that, but what can I do?

Just as Mom had hoped, more and more Dignityville residents have gotten involved in the garden. When they're not tilling or weeding, they sit around at meals and talk about what varieties of cabbage and beets to plant and what fertilizers to use. Meanwhile, Dad sold the Subaru to the junkyard, but a few days later developed a really bad toothache and had to go to the dentist. That was the end of the two hundred dollars. Easy come, easy go.

The good news is that he's gradually getting more involved in Dignityville–introducing an exercise program and giving his opinion when it comes to some of the political issues. Maybe, like Mom, it will be good for him to have something to latch on to, something that will help him feel productive and useful.

In fact, in Aubrey's absence, Mom and Dad have sort of become the ad hoc spokespeople for Dignityville. Residents come to them for advice, and when the town engineer decides to build a bike rack for all the donated bikes, he and Dad walk around looking for the right place to put it. When the mayor of another town comes to see the place, Mayor George asks Mom to give him a tour.

The downside is publicity. Two days ago the local paper did an article about Mom and the garden, and I think she's going to

9 **to till** to prepare land for growing crops, etc. – 10 **to weed** to remove wild, unwanted plants – 12 **junkyard** where old and unwanted things are kept and re-sold (*usu* in pieces) – 19 **to latch on to** to become interested in – 28 **downside** disadvantageous aspect

be interviewed by the TV station soon. So more and more people are learning that we live in Dignityville.

As a result I'm not just a promising high school pitcher anymore. Now I'm a *homeless* promising high school pitcher.

29

A MEETING

"It's not easy to get in touch with you."

"We lost our phone service."

"I'm sorry to hear that. Hopefully, if things work out, you'll get it back."

"How?"

"I know lots of people. We'll find you a job."

"What about the house?"

"You'll still get that, too. Think how much your family will appreciate it."

"You don't have to tell me. ... So what do you want me to do now?"

"Exactly what you've been doing. Gain their trust. Be their leader."

"And then?"

"When the time is right, I'll let you know."

"But no one else gets hurt. Swear it."

"I swear."

30

It's Saturday afternoon and I've just gotten back from my weekly run with Noah. In our tent Mom's sitting cross-legged, folding laundry. When Dad's not around these days, it could mean he's refereeing a baseball game, or it could mean he's collecting bottles and cans. Mom looks up. "Meg was just here."

Feeling awkward about leaving her so abruptly the night before, I go down to her tent and call in to her. When she comes out I can tell by the turmoil in her face that she must be feeling something similar.

"Can I ask you a really big favor?" she says. "Come to the hospital and talk to Aubrey?"

I try to keep the surprise off my face as she continues: "We're supposed to talk every day. It's important that he hears familiar voices. But it gets hard to think of things to say. It would be a big help."

By bike it's twenty minutes to the hospital, but I'll never get used to riding through town on two wheels. Bikes are for kids and grown-ups. Not teenage guys who should be cruising around in cars.

At the hospital the nurses, techs, and assistants wave or say hello like they know Meg, and I guess now that she's spent so much time here, most of them probably do.

Aubrey's room is decorated with posters of rock bands, Greenpeace, and a colorful one that says HATE-FREE ZONE. Framed photos of family and friends crowd the nightstand. Instead of a hospital blanket, the orange and blue bedspread looks like something from home. Aubrey's sitting back on a slant with eyes closed and tubes in his nose, mouth, and right arm, while his left is in a cast. His skin is deathly pale and there are scabs on his face where the scrapes and wounds from the beating

27 **slant** i.e. the bed is sloped so that he can sit up (or lie down when the slant is changed) – 29 **cast** hard case put over a broken bone *(Gips)* – 30 **scab** layer of dried blood on top of a wound – 30 **scrape** scratches *(Kratzer)*

have started to heal. He looks like he's asleep, only with neatly combed hair.

A radio is playing rock, a monitor is beeping, and the machine that helps him breathe wheezes robotically. I look back at Meg. "What do I say?"

"Anything. It's not what you say, it's the sound of your voice." She turns down the radio.

An unexpected tightness in my chest makes me realize I'm nervous. I'm not sure why it should feel so weird, but it does ... the idea of talking to someone in a coma. Meg comes closer. "Hey, Aubs, look who's here. You remember Dan." She gives me an encouraging nudge.

"So, uh, must be kind of a drag hanging out here all day," I begin. "Bet you really miss Dignityville, huh?" I mean it as a joke, but it doesn't work when the person you tell it to can't respond. I talk about Mom's garden, and how Dad's gotten involved in running things. Aubrey just lies there slack-jawed and unresponsive. I can see why Meg asked me to come. It's hard to imagine what she and her mom could possibly spend the hours talking to him about.

"So listen," I continue. "Know how we hear about machines replacing people and jobs being sent overseas? Get this: They're creating tables with screens for restaurants. So instead of a waiter, you pick from the menu on the screen. And you still get all the choices–rare, medium rare, well done, dressing on the side, no pickles–whatever you want. And after you place your order, they can estimate how long it'll take, so you don't have to sit around wondering. But here's the thing, what if half a million waiters and waitresses in this country get replaced by tables with screens and a bunch of minimum-wage busboys to serve meals and clean up? Even if the companies that make those tables create ten thousand new jobs, it's still a loss of four hundred and ninety thousand jobs."

12 **nudge** gentle push – 13 **a drag** *(sl)* sth that is tiresome – 17 **slack-jawed** open mouthed

Meg nods and smiles encouragingly.

"And the Chinese? They have factories with dormitories so the workers can live right on the premises," I continue. "If a rush order comes in the middle of the night, they wake up three hundred workers and within half an hour they're in production. So not only do they pay workers less over there, but they're way faster."

Meg's still smiling appreciatively.

"And that reminds me," I go on. "Do you know your sister's talking about skipping college and getting a job after high school?"

Meg widens her eyes at me and stops smiling.

"I mean, what's up with that?" I ask, now speaking to both of them. "You want her to be a waitress who's going to get replaced by a smart table? Or maybe she'll wind up in some factory dormitory getting up in the middle of the night to assemble widgets because that's the only way we can compete?"

Aubrey doesn't respond, of course, but Meg wrinkles her nose. "There are *other* kinds of work."

"Where you don't need a college education?" I challenge her. "School-bus driver? Construction? Lunch lady?"

Meg rolls her eyes dismissively.

"How do you like that?" I ask Aubrey. "She invites me here to talk and then doesn't like what I have to say." Then I have a brainstorm and look across the bed at Meg. "Hey, seriously? What about something in the medical field? I mean, considering how much time you spend here, right?"

Meg blinks and her expression crumbles.

Oh, crap … her dad's dying and her brother's in a coma. What was I thinking?

Her eyes start to glitter and she looks away. I feel horrible. "I didn't mean it that way. I–"

2 **dormitory** room with several beds for a group of people to sleep communally – 17 **widget** small mechanical device – 22 **dismissively** refusing to consider sth seriously

She leaves the bedside and presses her face into her hands.

I turn to Aubrey. "Listen, man, I know this is going to sound like sick coma humor, but I really hope you didn't hear any of that."

Meg sits down in the only chair in the room, so I have to kneel to her eye level. "Hey."

She's making those muffled, snuffling "I don't want you to see or hear me cry" sounds.

"I'm sorry. Really."

"I know." She nods without taking her hands from her face. "You didn't mean it that way. You just … have no idea what it's like."

"You're right. I'm trying to imagine, and at the same time I have this feeling that I'll never come close."

She lowers her hands and looks at me with reddened, teary eyes.

I take her in my arms and hold her. The only sounds are the beeps and rasps of the machines that are keeping her brother alive.

It's turning dark when we leave the hospital to ride our charity bikes back to Dignityville. The wind in our faces is supposed to be the sensation of freedom and possibilities, but at the moment the best we can hope for is not getting a bug in the eye.

We leave the bikes outside the tent that belongs to Joel, the heavyset guy with the bushy eyebrows and beard, who's appointed himself the Emperor of Bikes. He comes out and asks, "Everything okay?"

"Yeah, they worked fine."

Like Mom with her garden, he seems happy to have a purpose, fixing flats and straightening wheels. The stars are out, and as Meg and I walk down the dirt path, our swinging hands bump and I catch hers and hold it–not just because I think that she needs a boost, but because it feels good to be able to let my

33 **boost** encouragement, support

guard down and be close and share something … even if it's a downer.

We stop outside her tent, and the next thing I know, we're in each other's arms. She whispers, "Thank you, Dan."

"You don't have to thank me." We hug and share a quick impulsive kiss. Meg gives me a puzzled look that reflects the way I feel. A moment later I head slowly back to my tent, not sure why I just kissed her. Except that I felt like it.

Mom's inside reading her Zen gardening book by the lantern. She looks up, smiles, then must see something in my face. "What is it?"

Here's a strange question: Does homelessness bring families closer together? If we were still living in our house, I'd probably go up to my room and get online. But here we are in this tent. Who else is there to talk to?

So I lay out the whole situation. It sounds so lame. So much like the plot of a dumb movie no girl could ever get her boyfriend to watch.

See Dan, who's gotten involved with two girls.

See Dan have no idea what he's doing.

Run, Dan, run.

1 **downer** *here:* depressing

31

At school on Monday my situation with Talia and Meg is weighing on me. A guilty conscience says I'm being unfair to both of them.

At lunch Talia gestures to the spot she's saved at the table. As far as she's concerned, everything's great. We went to the movies with Noah and Tory on Saturday night. She doesn't know about my visit to the hospital earlier that day, or that on Sunday, while she was off doing dressage, Meg and I did homework together in the dining tent.

Talia smiles affectionately and presses close. Across from us Noah says, "Throwing today?"

"You bet."

We're just one big happy clique.

The conversations angle off in other directions–parties, college, cars. Only, according to Mom, I'm supposed to tell Talia privately that I need "some time off" to think and sort things out.

Yeah, right.

There's no situation in baseball that I'm afraid of. The more dire the scenario, the more I want to be on the mound, staring down the batter. I wouldn't care if Willie Mays was at the plate and my whole career was on the line.

But I can't be honest with Talia.

That afternoon my pitches are popping and I'm feeling good about the upcoming Thanksgiving tournament. Later, stopping at the Starbucks to use the Wi-Fi, I spot a familiar-looking head of half-black, half-orange-red hair. It's Detective French, sitting

1 **weighing** ['weɪɪŋ] **on me** making me worried – 19 **dire** ['daɪɚ] desperate – 19 **mound** [maʊnd] spot on baseball field where the pitcher pitches (throws) the ball to the batter – 20 **Willy Mays** one of the greatest baseball players of all time – 20 **plate** spot on baseball field where the batter stands in order to hit the ball – 23 **popping** *here:* going really well

at a table with a venti cup. I hesitate, but as if she senses a presence, she turns and sees me.

"Hi. I'm, uh, Meg Fine's friend." I approach.

Detective French blinks. No sign of comprehension.

"Her brother Aubrey got beat up behind Ruby's?"

It clicks. "Oh, yes. How is he?"

"Still in a coma."

She winces. "I'm sorry."

A beat passes. She glances at me again, as if thinking, *Is there a reason you're still here?*

"Could I have a moment?" I ask.

Her eyes narrow slightly, then she gestures to an empty chair. I sit and speak in a low voice. "So, I know investigations have to be confidential and everything, but I was just wondering if you'd had any luck?"

"Finding out who assaulted Aubrey?" There's something flat and defeated in her voice.

Obviously the news isn't good.

"You hear that the police department is going to lay off twenty-five percent of the force by year's end?" she asks.

I hadn't. "You?"

She shakes her head. "Thank God for seniority. But we'll go from five detectives to three. And our overtime's already been cut to nothing. You ask about your friend's brother? Let me ask *you* a question: Should solving that crime take precedence over tracking down a murderer, or rapist, or armed robber who might strike again?"

Welcome to Rhetorical Questions 101. Facing the obvious answer, I gaze away into space.

The guys who beat up Aubrey are going to get away with it.

Detective French studies me for a moment. I bet she feels bad. "Look, here's something else. How many outstanding warrants

1 **venti cup** the second largest drink size at Starbucks – 19 **to lay sb off** to end sb's employment status – 22 **seniority** superior status

do you think there are in Jefferson County right now? That means suspects whom the police have identified and are supposed to track down because they've been accused of committing a crime."

I shrug, not out of disrespect, but because I've got no basis for knowing.

"Okay, it's not a fair question," Detective French admits. "But here's the point. Take whatever number was in your head and multiply it by ten. So maybe the typical citizen thinks there are five hundred outstanding warrants? And now I'm saying that it's five thousand."

She pauses. I get the point. ... There are a lot of people out there who are wanted by the police.

"Now suppose I tell you the actual number is closer to *twenty-eight thousand*," she says. "That includes everything from failing to pay alimony or a parking ticket, all the way to rape and armed robbery. Of course, some bad guys have a lot more than one arrest warrant out on them. But think about it, Dan. Who's got the time to track down all those suspects? We didn't have the time to do it *before* they announced they were cutting the police force by twenty-five percent."

"So ... all those bad guys get away?"

Detective French gazes out the window. "Until they get pulled over for something stupid like driving with a broken taillight, and the computer IDs them. You ever wonder why they have those chases we love to watch on TV? Most of the time it's because the perp knows there's a warrant out for him, and as soon as the cops run his ID, he's going to go to jail. So why *not* make a run for it?"

"So no one's even *trying* to figure out who beat up Aubrey?"

The lines around Detective French's eyes deepen and she reaches into her bag, lifts out her iPad, and fires it up. "Here's

16 **alimony** money paid to your former wife or husband – 27 **perp** *(AE, abb)* perpetrator, criminal

what we've got. Witness states that there were three assailants, but it was dark and difficult to see. Police found gang beads at the scene." She looks at me. "Three perps come out of the dark, attack your friend, and vanish. The victim's in a coma so he can't provide any information. What are the chances of finding them?"

"So … that's it?" I'm still finding this hard to believe.

Detective French lets out a long, regretful sigh. "You want the truth? Unless something unusual happens? Yes, that's probably it." She finishes her venti, checks her watch, says she has to go. I thank her and stay at the table. There's homework to do.

But it isn't easy.

The police aren't even looking. …

I stew on it for a while, but the clock's ticking. My full ride at Rice is predicated on maintaining a certain grade average, so I force myself to study, and manage to finish a good chunk. By now it's getting dark and I'm packing up my stuff, when I see something out of the corner of my eye. A pickup truck across the street is slowly pulling away from the curb, and there's Dad on the sidewalk. In the dim light the pickup's red taillights move away down the street. They're old and narrow, not like the wraparound taillights on newer models.

Was it Mr. Purcellen's truck?

Did Dad just get out?

I can't be sure. Meanwhile, Dad starts walking in the direction of Dignityville.

In our tent Dad's sitting on one of the camping chairs, bent forward with his elbows on his knees, a deeply pensive look on his face as he stares at another small gauze bandage on his forearm. When he hears me come in, he nonchalantly rolls his sleeve down to cover it.

1 **assailant** person who attacks another person – 13 **stew on** *(inf) here:* think about – 14 **predicated on** dependent on – 15 **chunk** *(inf)* substantial amount – 21 **wraparound taillight** red light at the back of a car that goes around the sides – 28 **gauze** [gɑːz] **bandage** thin piece of cotton used for tying around a wound

My insides are a jumble. I know about the cans and bottles, but this is the second time I've seen a bandage over the vein where they take blood. If he were sick, I'd know because Mom would be doing her best Florence Nightingale. So that leaves one other possibility: He's selling it to a blood bank.

"You okay?" I ask.

"Sure. Just … uh, thinking."

I can't ask him about the blood, but I can about something else. "Did you just get out of Mr. Purcellen's pickup over by Starbucks?"

Dad stiffens, then shakes his head. "No."

"That's weird. I thought I saw the pickup, and then you were standing there."

"I was just taking a walk."

Or coming back from selling blood.

My stomach grumbles. "Want to get some dinner?"

It's a simple question, yet Dad gazes off and seems to ponder it thoughtfully.

"Hello?"

He looks back, a blank expression on his face. This isn't like him.

"You *sure* you're okay?" I ask.

He nods. "Go ahead. I'll be there in a little while."

I head over to the dining tent. Mom's sitting with Mona, Stella, Fred, and Diane. It's like even here in Dignityville we've got our own little clique. I get in the food line, not really paying attention, my thoughts still on what happened back at Starbucks.

As I get close to the servers, I check what's for dinner. Looks like lasagna, which is good because it's one of those meals that's hard to mess up. I slide my tray and look up … into Tory's eyes.

She's a volunteer server tonight.

I feel my face go hot and red. It's like standing here naked. But then, surprisingly, the embarrassment passes. *What*

1 **jumble** in a mixed and disordered way – 4 **Florence Nightingale** (1820–1910), British nurse, founder of modern western nursing

difference does it make? She already knows, right? She smiles sympathetically and starts to dig into the lasagna with a serving spoon.

"Whoa!" I raise a hand to stop her. "Did Noah and Zach have anything to do with making this?"

Her face scrunches with curiosity. "No."

"You positive?"

"It was donated by Alfredo's in town. Why?"

"Just making sure." I lower my hand. "Those two guys are not to be trusted in a kitchen."

"I'll, uh, keep that in mind." Tory smiles, then lowers her voice while she dumps a square on my plate. "It's really good. I snuck a little when no one was watching."

"Tsk, tsk. Stealing from the homeless?" I tease.

She holds up her thumb and forefinger about an inch apart. "It only was this much."

"I'll let you get away with it this time," I jokingly warn. "But do it again and you won't be allowed back, understand?"

Tory pretends to shake with fear, and salutes. "Yes, sir!"

We share a grin and a wink, and I head off. Truth is, that wasn't nearly as bad as I might have imagined. When I return to our table, Fred has to greet me with his latest joke: "What's a frog's favorite soft drink?"

"I don't know, Fred, what?" I ask.

"Croaka-Cola."

I groan. Stella giggles with delight, which makes Mona, Diane, and Mom smile.

We're just one little happy homeless family, I think.

Dad never shows up for dinner.

12 **square** *i.e.* his meal: a square piece of lasagna – 12 **to sneak, snuck, snuck** to secretly take sth

32

"Make it your community issues project," Ms. Mitchell says the next day in the library when we run into each other. I've just brought up what Detective French told me about wanted criminals going free because the police don't have the time or manpower to track them down.

Oh, man, why did I have to open my big mouth?

"Don't roll your eyes, Mr. Halprin," my government and politics teacher scolds good-naturedly. "Everyone has to do a project this semester. At least you'll have one you're interested in."

Guess she's got a point.

Later I run into Meg in the hall. According to Mom, I'm supposed to tell *her* I need some time off. But I know I won't, just like I couldn't tell Talia. Not for the same reason, though. I won't tell Meg because I can't stand the idea of hurting her.

"Hey." She smiles warmly, and we start to walk together. I'm equal parts glad to be with her and nervous about which of Talia's friends is going to see us.

"I just wanted to say thanks," she says.

"For?"

"Caring about Aubrey."

"How is he?"

Her shoulders hunch. "No change. The test scores aren't getting worse, but he still hasn't woken up."

Once again I want to put my arms around her to comfort her, but I hesitate, thinking of Talia and her spies.

You can't live like this, Dan.

So I put my arm around her anyway.

22 **to hunch** to draw up together (she is shrugging her shoulders to show that she is disappointed)

33

A MEETING

"You're going to start a rumor and organize a protest at Town Hall. The idea is to get everyone out of Dignityville for a short period of time."

"No."

"Listen carefully. It's going to happen whether you like it or not. If you truly don't want anyone to get hurt, you'll get them out of there."

"If you do anything to Dignityville, I'll tell the police."

"And they'll find out that you conspired to have Aubrey Fine beaten."

"That's a lie."

"Prove it."

"You son of a bitch."

"I don't think you recognize the magnitude of all this, Mr. Halprin. There are people in this town who have millions and millions invested in real estate. There are banks holding *tens* of millions of dollars in real estate and construction loans. It all comes down to one very simple thing: the value of property. If real estate values fall, investors can't sell or rent their properties for enough money to pay back their loans. Do you know what happens then?"

"The investors forfeit the properties and the banks get stuck with them."

"Correct. And in the process, not only do the investors lose a great deal of money, but the people who work for them lose their jobs. Architects, construction workers, cement suppliers, carpenters, plumbers, electricians, bricklayers, real estate

9 **to conspire** to plan sth illegal – 22 **forfeit** ['fɔːrfət] lose (because payments were not met – the investor here is a person or family that lives in the house) – 27 **plumber** ['plʌmɚ] person that installs and repairs water pipes, drains, etc

brokers, title companies, building superintendents, doormen, janitors ... hundreds and hundreds of people become unemployed. And it doesn't stop there, Mr. Halprin, because eventually the banks with bad loans either go out of business or have to consolidate with other banks, and that means the layoffs of tellers and loan officers and appraisers. And do you know what that means?"

"The unemployed have less money to spend on food and clothes, so restaurants and stores go out of business."

"Precisely. And when the people who worked in those restaurants and stores become unemployed, *they* have no money to spend, and that leads to more businesses closing, and it becomes one gigantic downward spiral. That's why your wife lost her job as a stockbroker. It wasn't that she performed poorly, it was just that people no longer had the money to invest in stocks. And even *that's* not the end of it, because when businesses close and people become unemployed, they stop paying taxes. Do you know what the cities of Vallejo, California; Central Falls, Rhode Island; Birmingham, Alabama; and Harrisburg, Pennsylvania, all have in common?"

"They've gone bankrupt."

"Correct again, Mr. Halprin. And when a city goes bankrupt, it has to lay off police and firemen and teachers. That makes the city less attractive to people who want a safe place to live and good schools for their children. And that sends property values even lower. If you bought a house in Vallejo, California, in 2006 for a hundred thousand dollars, do you know what that house was worth four years later?"

"Seventy thousand dollars?"

"Try thirty-three thousand dollars. You lost sixty-seven thousand dollars on your investment. And the whole giant spiral

1 **title company** firm that deals with documents of ownership – 5 **to consolidate** to unite or combine – 6 **teller** a bank employee who receives and pays out money – 6 **loan officer** bank employee who approves/disapproves the amount of money you want to borrow – 6 **appraiser** person who sets a value on a piece of property

of dropping property values leading to more unemployment leading to bankruptcy leading to ever lower property values continues."

"Why should I care? I've already lost everything."

"Not quite, Mr. Halprin. You have a son who needs a scholarship to go to college next year. There are several wealthy investors in this town who also went to Rice, and who make a habit of giving substantial monetary gifts to their alma mater each year. Needless to say, Daniel's scholarship is by no means a certainty."

"You ... you ... ruthless bastard."

"Not if you look at it in terms of the greatest good for the largest number of people, Mr. Halprin. In the short run, perhaps a hundred already homeless people will be displaced. But in the long run, many hundreds, possibly even thousands, of jobs and families and homes will be preserved. Median will continue to be an active, thriving community of residents who are happy to live here, instead of a decaying, bankrupt dumping ground of abandoned houses and boarded-up stores."

Silence.

"I need an answer, Mr. Halprin. Are you going to organize that protest or not?"

Silence.

"Mr. Halprin?"

"I can probably get most of them out, but what about the ones who can't be moved?"

"I'll need to know exactly which tents they're in."

8 **monetary gift** financial present, donation – 9 **by no means** absolutely not – 17 **thriving** flourishing, growing – 18 **decaying** falling apart, getting poorer – 19 **boarded up** covered with wood, closed

34

In the library, Googling open arrest warrants, I discover a dark secret. A lot of states don't bother to keep records of how many criminals they've failed to track down and arrest. Probably because they don't want anyone to know how easy it is to get away with crime. But according to the state attorney general of California, the number in that state alone is–ready for this?–*2.5 million* outstanding warrants.

That includes 252,000 outstanding felony warrants for serious "Your butt is going to jail" crimes, including 2,800 for homicide, 640 for kidnapping, and 1,800 for sexual assault.

Warrants mean the police know *who* those criminals are, so I have to assume they just don't know *where* they are. And they don't have the money or time or manpower to find them.

If they can't track down criminals whose identities are *known*, what are the chances of them tracking down the three *unknown* assailants who beat up Aubrey?

Welcome to the United States of Part-Time Law Enforcement.

"Dan?"

I look up from the computer into Talia's distraught, watery eyes. She pulls a chair up and sits hugging herself as if she has a stomachache. "What's going on? You were walking down the hall with your arm around Meg?"

Her network of spies rivals the CIA's.

I explain that Meg needed comforting.

"Why does she have to get it from you?" Talia asks with dismay.

"Uh, maybe because we have something in common?"

Using her pinky, she carefully draws a tear out of her eye without smearing her makeup. She's waiting for me to reach out, tell her she's the one I truly care for. But something stops

5 **attorney** [ə'tɜ:rni] **general** *(AE)* chief law officer of a state – 7 **outstanding** not settled, unresolved – 8 **felony** *(usu AE)* serious crime such as murder – 9 **homicide** ['hɑ:məsaɪd] murder; the killing of one human being by another – 17 **law enforcement** ensuring that laws are followed – 19 **distraught** [dɪ'strɑ:t] very upset (e.g. from worry or sadness)

me. Maybe it's knowing deep down that it'll only prolong this crazy situation.

When I don't react, Talia's face goes stony. Without a word she gets up and leaves.

I feel a forlorn regret that weighs down on my shoulders and compresses my heart. This time she won't be back. We're through.

In the locker room after school I borrow Noah's phone, then go into a stall. His brother's studio is on speed dial.

"Hello?" a female voice answers.

"Olivia?"

"Who's this?"

"Dan Halprin, Noah's friend?"

"Oh my God, Dan, how are you? What's up? When are you coming down to the studio again?"

After taking a few moments to catch up, I get to the point: "Is all that talk about Buzzuka Joe once being a gangbanger true, or just hype?"

"As far as I know it's true. Why?"

"What about Oscar?"

"Tell me what you need, Dan."

I tell her about Aubrey's beating and the gang beads and the police being unable to find out who did it. "I know there's no reason why Buzzuka Joe should know anything about it, but I don't know anyone else who's even remotely connected to that world. ..."

The connection goes quiet, as if Olivia's thinking. "He'll be in the studio to do some mixes today. I can't promise anything, but I'll ask."

Later, back at Dignityville, there's a buzz in the air. Hunched over a bike in front of his tent, Joel sees me and says, "Aubrey woke up."

5 **forlorn** miserable – 27 **mix** electronic blending of music to produce a recording

Outside the Fines' tent, an old gray-haired guy in a chair raises his hand cautiously, then speaks in a low voice as if he doesn't want Meg's dad inside to hear. "They're both at the hospital. We're keeping an eye on Sam until they get back."

As I head back up the path, I notice Dad in the dining tent with a group of people, and wonder if he's heard the good news. But getting closer, I can tell that they're discussing something serious. "Sorry, didn't mean to interrupt." I join them.

Wade, the guy with the long gray ponytail, turns to Dad and says, "Shouldn't you tell him? I mean, it's already been on the news."

Dad bites his lip indecisively, but Wade decides for him. "There was another attack this morning," he says gravely. "Well, at least, an *attempted* attack. She managed to get away, but they grabbed her and said some pretty nasty things."

"Who?" I ask.

Wade glances at Dad.

"A woman from here," Dad says. "She's really shaken up. Doesn't want anyone to know who she is."

"Where'd it happen?" I ask.

"The Stop and Shop," Wade says.

"We're taking it to Town Hall," says a woman named Sarah with short white hair, piercings, and sleeves of tattoos on both arms. "The homeless need more protection."

"It's going to be an entirely peaceful, nonviolent demonstration," Dad quickly adds.

Leaving the dining tent, I'm blindsided by a pair of arms that wrap around my neck. For one alarmed instant I think I'm being taken down by attackers, but it's Meg, and her embrace is one of joy.

"He's awake!" she cries happily. "Oh, Dan!" She squeezes so hard she practically chokes me, then plants a big kiss on my cheek. "He's talking and moving and everything!" Tears of happiness drip down her face. "Will you come see him? Tomorrow after school?"

Her elation is contagious. It's hard to imagine anyone being happier.

"Definitely," I answer.

With a mile-wide smile she kisses me again, then breaks away. "Mom's still at the hospital. I've got to go check on Dad. See you tomorrow!" She dashes off toward her tent, half running, half skipping.

1 **elation is contagious** joyfulness is catching

35

The next morning when I tell Noah I can't make our workout that afternoon, he's understandably annoyed.

"Today's the exception. Aubrey woke up. I have to go to the hospital to see him."

Noah sighs as if to say, *I knew it wouldn't last. All talk and no follow-through.*

The tension may begin with Noah, but it doesn't end there. I'm surprised to find Talia waiting at my locker with a somber expression.

"Can we talk later?" she asks. "I have a yearbook meeting at lunch, but I could do it right after school."

I can't imagine what she wants to say, but we were together for two years. I owe it to her.

In government and politics Meg smiles warmly and gives me a happy little wave. I hope she'll understand when I tell her I'll get to the hospital a little late this afternoon.

Ms. Mitchell waddles in, her face flushed as usual. But instead of going to her desk, she stops in front of the class. "Anyone see the *Median Buzz* this morning?"

No one responds.

"So you haven't heard about the protest?" she asks.

"You mean the homeless march on Washington?" Ben asks.

"No, I mean right here," Ms. Mitchell replies. "There's going to be a demonstration at Town Hall for more police protection for the homeless."

When half the class turns and looks at me, Ms. Mitchell realizes why. Instead of pretending otherwise, she follows their lead. "Well, Dan, how do you feel about it?"

At this point being singled out doesn't bother me anymore. "I'm in favor of more police protection for everyone."

8 **somber** dark, very serious – 17 **to waddle** [ˈwɑːdəl] to walk with short steps like a duck

Ms. Mitchell chuckles. "Thank you for that glib reply, Dan. I'm sure it was deeply heartfelt." Having drenched me with sarcasm, she looks for someone else.

But she's right. So why not say what's really on my mind? "Okay, seriously? That protest may be happening here, but for most of the kids in this school it might as well be in another country."

Ms. Mitchell studies me. "You sound angry."

Yeah, well, it's hard not to be. I still can't put my mother's positive "pioneer" spin on Dignityville. "Try humiliated and embarrassed. It's like everyone thinks there's something wrong with you."

I catch myself and stop, startled by what I've just blurted out. But now everyone in class is looking at me and I feel the urge to go on. "But that's not the worst part. Want to know what the worst is? The hopelessness. Not for me, but for my parents … and all the other ones around their age? Like never being able to get jobs again doing what they used to do. I mean, for so many people there's nothing to look forward to."

Silence, and that slightly eerie, unexpected feeling when you realize they're actually listening. Ben nods like maybe there's something other than rosin in my skull after all. Ms. Mitchell clears her throat. "Thank you for sharing that with us, Dan. I know it can't have been easy, and we all appreciate it."

She invites other opinions, and the GPA zombies leap at the opportunity to score class-participation points. I'm still finding it difficult to believe that I just vented so publicly about something so private. Has my body been taken over by aliens from Planet Emo?

In the hall after class Meg has an earnest expression, like she's going to say something about how impressed she was that I spoke out.

2 **drenched** *here:* covered, filled – 13 **to blurt out** to utter impulsively – 20 **eerie** strange and scary – 22 **rosin** *Harz* – 27 **to vent** *(AE)* to express one's thoughts forcefully – 29 **Planet Emo** place where emo's live

But I've got something I need to tell her. "Listen, about this afternoon ..."

"You can't come?" Her face falls.

"I can. But I have to take care of something else first. It shouldn't take long."

That earns a half smile, and she says, "I can wait."

"It would be better if you didn't."

Good-bye half smile. As if she knows it must have something to do with Talia, she slides her eyes away. "Okay, then I'll see you there, I guess."

For some reason I can't just spin on my heels and go off toward my next class. Something makes me want to give her spirits a lift, so I place my hand on hers and gently squeeze. "I promise."

I don't expect the meeting with Talia to go very long. I mean, what's there to talk about once she tells me that she's thought it over and realized that we've grown apart and we're not the same people that we used to be and she'll always remember the good times we had?

School ends and I dawdle inside for a few minutes while the herd heads for greener pastures. When I do get outside, a couple of small groups are hanging around talking, while a few others wait at the curb for rides. Talia's by the flagpole, the strap of her book bag over her shoulder. I walk over, tempted to say, *Listen, this isn't necessary. Let's just shake hands and part friends.*

Except Talia says, "I don't want it to end like this, Dan."

Does she mean that she wants it to end, but in a different way? No, that's not what she means.

"I care too much about you." Looking up into my eyes, she moves closer.

I'm completely flummoxed. "I ... I care about you, too, Tal."

19 **to dawdle** ['dɑːdəl] to take one's time – 30 **flummoxed** ['flʌməkst] confused, puzzled

She slides her arms around my waist and hugs, but I'm still in shock. This is so *not* what I anticipated. But at least I was truthful. I *do* care about her. I'm just not sure it's the kind of caring she's talking about.

"I know you've been going through a really rough time," she says, still hugging me. "I just never imagined that things could get this ... this extreme." She presses her cheek against my shoulder, which is good because she can't see the stunned expression that must be on my face. The sweet scent of her perfume brings back lots of pleasant memories. Meanwhile I'm totally reexamining the past. Does the fact that she's paid for everything we've done for months show a greater degree of understanding and sympathy than I've been willing to admit?

And she's done all the driving and paid for all the gas. And never once complained about any of it.

An unsettled feeling envelops me. Have I been totally unfair and judgmental, and maybe just plain wrong? With Talia in no rush to let go, I glance around to make sure Meg didn't stay after school to see what my delay was.

No, she's not that kind of person.

Talia raises her head. "Who are you looking for?"

"Uh, no one." Who am I trying to fool? She's way smarter than that.

She leans back and studies me. "What's going on with you and that girl?"

"I told you, Tal. We have things in common."

"But you're not ... involved with her, are you?"

I shake my head.

"You *sure*?"

I nod, even though I'm not sure of anything. Talia relaxes and seems mollified. "Can I give you a ride?"

I point back at the school entrance. "Gotta practice with Noah."

16 **unsettling** worrying, troubling – 17 **judgmental** criticizing people very quickly – 31 **mollified** calmed, pacified

"Okay." She stretches up and kisses me. "Talk to you later." She bounces away, clearly pleased that we're still a couple.

Why can't I be honest with her?

Is it really that hard to give her up?

Or is it just hard to give up what she represents?

At the hospital Meg gives me a crooked smile as if she's torn between her joy for her brother's recovery and her concern over why I couldn't leave right after school to see him. I shoot her a cheerful nod even though inside I'm blown away by what just happened with Talia.

Aubrey's sitting up in bed with a blue cast on his left arm and an iPad on his lap. He looks gaunt and pale. The tubes have been removed from his mouth and nose, but are still in his right arm.

"How are you?" I ask.

"Okay," he answers in a hoarse whisper, as if his voice is rusty from lack of use. "I'm awake." But the effort to say those few words seems to tire him.

I gesture to the iPad. "Nice."

"It's not his," Meg says. "A nurse here's letting him use it."

"Not like … I'm going anywhere with it," Aubrey quips, then waits expectantly.

So I grin. "Good one."

He grins back and I sense he's relieved. As if my reaction means that he still has a sense of humor. But now the smile disappears and he looks serious. He slowly inches the iPad in my direction. On the screen is the *Median Buzz*'s home page with a headline:

RUMORS OF COUNTERPROTEST GROW

I skim the story about opposition gathering against the demonstration for more police protection. It's the same argument we heard at the Town Hall meeting: The homeless don't pay any taxes. What right do they have to demand more than anyone else?

12 **gaunt** [gɑːnt] thin – 20 **to quip** to joke

"How did they know … she was homeless?" Aubrey asks, referring to the woman who was threatened at the Stop and Shop.

"The same way they knew you were homeless, I guess."

Aubrey's forehead furrows. "Who knew?"

I glance at Meg, wondering what she's told him about the attack. She looks wary. Aubrey sees this. "Tell me."

"You were attacked in the parking lot behind Ruby's," she says. "I told you, remember? The baseball bat? That's why you were in a coma."

Aubrey blinks as if this is all new information, but people often can't remember traumatic experiences. "What did … she say happened?"

"I don't know. She doesn't want to talk about it."

His eyebrows rise and dip with consternation. "But she told … someone."

"My dad. He's the only one who knows who she is."

Aubrey's eyes dip further. "*You* … don't know who she is?"

"No one except my dad."

Meg's brother goes silent and looks away. Several moments pass before he says, "Don't demonstrate."

It's hard to know how to take this. Is he thinking clearly? As if he senses this concern, he takes a deep breath. "They attacked me … because they wanted to. … It was deliberate." He closes his eyes and sighs as if this conversation is taking way too much energy.

"Maybe we should drop it," Meg suggests protectively.

"No," Aubrey insists. "If there's violence, it's going to polarize … give the other side a reason … to feel threatened." He leans back in bed and closes his eyes again.

"Maybe it's time to go, Dan," Meg says softly.

Aubrey opens his eyes. "I'm not … finished."

5 **to furrow** *here:* to form deep lines in your skin – 24 **deliberate** [dɪˈlɪbᵊrət] intentional, done on purpose

"We can talk about it another time." Meg's clearly worried that he's stressing too much.

But her brother perseveres. "It'll scare people away from Dignityville. … They'll be afraid … of more violence."

That makes sense. But my father's in favor of the demonstration. I have to think carefully about this.

This time when Aubrey closes his eyes, they stay closed. Meg tilts her head toward the door and raises a finger as if I should wait for her. A moment later she joins me in the hallway.

"It's posttraumatic amnesia," she whispers. "He forgets things. In a few minutes he may not even remember what we just talked about."

"But when he does remember, it seems like he thinks pretty clearly," I whisper back. "How long does he have to stay here?"

"It depends. They've started him on physical therapy to get his strength and balance back. But he still has a long way to go." She glances into the room. Aubrey's reclined in his bed, his eyes still closed. I take her hand and squeeze it. When she looks up at me, her eyes are watery and she blinks back the tears. "Thanks for coming," she croaks, then turns away down the hall so I won't see her cry.

When I leave the hospital in the dark, I discover that the back tire on the bike I used has gone flat. By the time I walk it back to Dignityville, they've stopped serving dinner. Spaghetti was on the menu tonight, but the servers and big pots are gone. All that's left are some pats of butter and stale bread.

With a plate of bread and butter, I find Dad at one of the dining tables, looking gloomy. I wonder what he's been doing all day. Organizing the demonstration at Town Hall? Collecting bottles and cans? Selling blood?

"Where've you been?" he asks.

3 **to persevere** [ˌpɜːrsəˈvɪr] to keep on, to refuse to stop – 8 **tilts** rolls, points – 10 **posttraumatic amnesia** loss of memory immediately following a traumatic event

I'm about to tell him about Aubrey when I hear a heated conversation nearby. Mom, dressed in her gardening clothes, is talking to a man wearing a plaid shirt and overalls. I can't hear what they're saying, but the crossed arms and clenched jaws cry out disagreement.

"Mutiny in the cabbage patch," Dad mutters.

"The cucumbers don't want to be planted next to the string beans?" I ask.

He isn't amused. "It's serious."

I glance again at Mom and Farmer Joe or whoever he is. Now there's just silence between them. With glittering eyes, Mom abruptly turns away and comes toward us, sitting down hard. When she picks up her carry mug to take a sip of tea, her hand is shaking. "I've always used organic fertilizer. I know it's more expensive and that inorganic produces a slightly better yield. But this garden was my idea. I fought for it and now he comes out of nowhere with his 'What do women know about farming?' routine." She balls her hands into fists. "Oh, I'd like to kill him!"

Dad covers one of her hands in his. Mom dabs her eyes and looks at my plate of bread and butter. "Where's your dinner?"

"I got here too late."

Her eyebrows dip into a *V*, as if she wants to figure out how to solve this problem, but then she sighs sadly, as if realizing she can't. "Do you want to get Subway?"

I would, but I don't want to spend the money. "It's okay. I had a really big lunch," I lie, hoping the bread will be enough to get me through tonight.

Mom accepts this. "So how was your day, sweetheart?"

"I saw Aubrey. You know he woke up?"

She manages to smile. "Yes."

I take a breath, rub my hands together, and tell Dad what Aubrey said about the demonstration being a mistake.

6 **mutiny** ['mju:tᵊni] open rebellion – 6 **cabbage patch** *Kohlkopfbeet* – 7 **cucumber** ['kju:kʌmbɚ] *Gurke* – 7 **string bean** type of long thin green bean – 19 **dabs her eyes** brushes away a tear (she's crying)

He nods gravely. "He may be right, but I still think we have to do it."

"How can you say that if you think he's right?" I ask.

"There might be some opposition," Dad explains, "but as long as we keep things peaceful, it should be fine."

"How do you know you'll be able to keep it peaceful?" I ask.

"I think we will."

"How can you be sure?"

Dad sets his jaw firmly. "Dan, this is something I have to do."

But I don't understand. "Why?"

Instead of answering, he stares up at the ceiling of the dining tent and rakes his fingers back across his scalp. Without another word he gets up and stomps away, leaving his dinner half-eaten.

That is so not like him. I give Mom a quizzical look.

"Stress," she says, then slides her eyes to the table where Farmer Joe is sitting with some other men, talking. I can't help but wonder … is her pioneer spirit finally fading?

9 **sets his jaw** makes a grim, determined expression with his face – 14 **quizzical** questioning or puzzled

36

It's dark and I'm still in my sleeping bag. I listen to my parents' breathing–Dad's light snore, Mom's whiffs of exhalation. I've been sleeping in this tent for weeks and it still surprises me every morning when I wake and realize where I am. But this morning there are other sensations as well–hunger and dread. Last night, maybe for the first time in my life, I went to bed hungry and was kept awake for a long time while my stomach growled for food. Now I wish I had signed up for free school breakfasts as well as lunch.

Tonight's the demonstration at Town Hall. I can't shake this ominous feeling that something bad is going to happen. But what can I do? Dad's determined to go through with it. I slide out of the sleeping bag, quietly get dressed, and head out for school and something to eat.

***

I manage to sleepwalk through my classes until government and politics, where Ms. Mitchell fires up the SMART Board and projects the front page of the *Median Buzz*. The headlines read:

POLICE REPORT: NO EVIDENCE OF SECOND HOMELESS ATTACK

OPPOSITION TO DEMONSTRATION GROWS

MAYOR GEORGE ASKS BOTH SIDES TO STAY HOME

"Who wants to go first?" she asks.

While the usual suspects raise their hands, I'm wondering what's going on. *No evidence of the second attack?*

2 **whiff of exhalation** quiet sound of breathing out – 11 **ominous** threatening

"So the police are saying the second incident never took place?" Justin auto-tech troll asks.

"Let's just say they've cast doubt on it," replies Ms. Mitchell.

"Then what's the point of the demonstration tonight?" asks Susan Barrow.

Ms. Mitchell lifts her chin and looks around the room. I raise my hand. "If Mayor George wants to stop the demonstration, what would prevent him from having the police department issue that statement just to put doubt in people's minds?"

"You're saying the mayor and the police are lying, Dan?" Ben asks, but not in a condescending way.

"No, I'm saying that we don't know how deeply they investigated the second attack," I reply. "Maybe they just didn't look hard enough."

The United States of Part-Time Law Enforcement …

Quiet in the classroom. And now that I think about it, I can't help seeing Ben's point. If there really had been a second attack, how could the mayor and police pretend there hadn't been?

The victim never came forward.

Dad said the only person she'd confided in was him.

When class ends, Ms. Mitchell asks me to stay behind. Now what? Is she going to ask me to do a special report on the demonstration tonight?

She waits until the last student has left the room. "Dan, I want you to know how impressed I am."

Huh?

She continues: "I know this has been an extremely difficult experience for you, but what you may not realize is that it's probably been a very valuable one as well. You're not the same person you were when school began. You've become more thoughtful, and caring, and introspective. Even if you don't say another word between now and the end of the semester, I'll still probably give you an A."

31 **introspective** inward-looking, reflective – 33 **an A** the best grade in American schools

I usually don't see Noah until lunch in the cafeteria, so when I find him waiting for me at my locker, I know something's up. "I said I'd be there this afternoon," I assure him. "No way I'm missing two workouts in a row."'

"It's not that." He hands me an envelope. "Tory asked me to give this to you. She didn't want to do it in front of everyone at lunch."

Inside the envelope is a coupon book for free food at any Pizza Grandé. A few weeks ago I might have been riled, but not after last night, when I went to bed hungry. I slide the envelope into my pocket. "Thanks, man."

"Thank Tory," Noah says.

At lunch I catch her eye and nod my appreciation silently. She smiles briefly, then looks away before Talia or anyone else notices. A few moments later Noah squints down at his lap. His phone's vibrating, and with raised eyebrows, he passes it under the table to me and mouths Oscar's name.

The table goes quiet, knowing that if a lunch monitor catches us, Noah risks losing his phone. Talia gives me a concerned look. "Back in a sec," I whisper. The band room across the hall from the cafeteria is empty and I squeeze into a corner where I won't be seen.

Redial.

"This Dan?" Oscar answers.

"Yeah."

He tells me where to be at seven o'clock tonight. But that will be in the middle of the demonstration. "Can we do it another time?"

Oscar grunts, "You kidding me?" as if just setting this meeting was a herculean endeavor.

So that's my choice: go to the demonstration, where I'll be one in the crowd, or have a real opportunity to get some information about who beat up Aubrey.

9 **riled** a little angry – 15 **to squint** to look with your eyes partly closed – 30 **herculean** needing great strength and determination

"See you later."

Crossing the hall to the cafeteria, I spot Mason sitting alone at the march on Washington sign-up table, reading a book. Now that I think of it, he's been alone the last few times I've passed. On the wall behind him a corner of one of the posters has come unstuck and folds over.

"How's it going?" I ask.

He looks up from the book, *The Grapes of Wrath*–right, he's a junior; we read it last year. He gestures at the empty table. "Can't you tell? It's a mob scene."

I nod at the book. "Kind of timely, huh?"

"Scary timely. Listen." He flips to a folded-down page and reads: "'Fear the time when the strikes stop while the great owners live–for every little beaten strike is proof that the step is being taken ... fear the time when Manself will not suffer and die for a concept, for this one quality is the foundation of Manself, and this one quality is man, distinctive in the universe.'"

I tap the half-empty sign-up sheet. "Think the time to fear has come?"

He shrugs. "Unless they're homeless and hungry themselves, most people just don't care. ... How're *you* doing?"

"Hangin' in."

"Must be like the Weedpatch Camp over there, huh?" He gestures to the book.

"Guess so ... strange, isn't it? That book was written seventy or eighty years ago, and here we are again. At least, some of us." My eyes meet his and I wonder if anyone who isn't living in Dignityville can really truly understand. Then I get the answer.

Mason leans forward. "We've got this little two-bedroom apartment over our garage? It's just sitting there. I've been talking to my parents about letting someone use it. It doesn't seem right to leave it empty when people are in need, you know?"

10 **mob scene** criminal gang activity – 15 **Manself** term used by Steinbeck in *The Grapes of Wrath* expressing self-confidence that cannot be taken away – 23 **Weedpatch Camp** built in 1936 to house migrant workers in California

37

While Noah drives me back to Dignityville that afternoon, I can't help thinking about Mason's offer. I hate the idea that my family has gotten to the point where people are offering charity, but at the same time I really appreciate the fact that others are willing to help. His parents have nothing to gain by letting us stay in their spare apartment. It's simply from the goodness of their hearts.

But it's soon obvious that not everyone feels generous toward the homeless. In town Noah and I are sent on a detour. Lining police barricades are people with signs that say: GET A JOB, OCCUPY A DESK, YOU WANT SOCIALISM? MOVE TO SPAIN, OCCUPY REALITY, REAL PEOPLE WORK.

What's surprising is how many there are. Can they all be from Median? Has the news about tonight's demonstration spread that quickly?

A few blocks away the crowd of pro-homeless demonstrators has spilled onto the sidewalk outside Dignityville. Their signs read: POLICE PROTECTION FOR ALL, THE HOMELESS ARE HUMANS TOO, WE WANT TO WORK—WHERE ARE THE JOBS?

Dad's on the sidewalk with a megaphone, warning the crowd not to react to taunts from the opposition: "This is a nonviolent protest. No matter what they say, no matter what they do, do not respond, do not engage. Our intention is not to change the minds of those who are against us. We're going there to make a point to the mayor and town council."

In the car Noah gives my thigh a supportive slap. "Good luck. Don't get hurt."

I get out and work my way through the crowd to Dad, who's huddling with Wade and Joel.

"Dad?" I tap him on the back.

He turns, looking grim and determined. "Hey."

9 **detour** a roundabout way – 21 **taunt** [tɑːnt] sarcastic remark; insult

"Can we talk for a second?"

"Now? I'm in the middle–"

"It's superimportant."

He asks Wade and Joel to wait. In a low voice I tell him the police don't believe there was a second incident.

"I heard that. They're wrong," Dad states flatly.

Knowing that everyone from Dignityville is supposed to be here, I gesture to the crowd. "Where is she?"

His face reddens. "She … doesn't want to be identified."

"I swear I won't tell a soul."

We stare at each other. Is he not answering because he's realizing that I know any answer he gives will be a lie?

I finally ask, "Why, Dad?"

He looks everywhere but at me. "We'll talk … later."

"You know there's a mob in town waiting for you? I'm not sure they're all from around here."

"We've heard."

Mona and Stella are in the crowd from Dignityville, and so are one or two mothers with kids in strollers who must have moved in more recently. "You *sure* you want to do this, Dad?"

"I don't want to," he replies somberly. "I have to."

By the time the demonstration begins, I'm standing many blocks away on an empty corner in the dark, waiting and feeling nervous. Since Oscar's involved, I don't think I'm in any danger, but I'm still wondering if this is the right thing to do.

The Range Rover pulls up and Oscar lowers the window. "Get in."

I do as I'm told.

It's not long before we enter a sketchy neighborhood on the outskirts of Burlington–boarded-up storefronts, empty lots strewn with garbage and rubble, row houses with bars over the

19 **stroller** *(AE)* baby buggy – 21 **somberly** sad and seriously – 29 **sketchy** potentially dangerous – 30 **lot** piece of land – 31 **row** [roʊ] **house** *(AE)* terraced house *(Reihenhaus)*

windows and doors. Oscar pulls to the curb in front of a row of low, dark buildings and cuts the engine.

It's a quiet block. Lights are on in some of the houses. Others are dark. Now and then a car passes, but there's hardly anyone out on the sidewalks. Oscar sits quietly while I fight the urge to fidget.

We wait. …

Oscar harrumphs. "You ever wonder why this Dignityville thing is mostly about the white middle class and not folks from the hood?"

"Tell me."

"We know the score … known it since the day we stepped off the slave ship. Why pay a free white man an honest wage to pick cotton when you could get an African slave to do it for nothing? They call it free enterprise … and for two hundred years it ain't changed. It's still about paying the peons at the bottom less than they deserve so that the fat cats at the top can keep more than they need."

"Amen, brother."

Oscar smirks. "Yeah, *you* know. The only difference now is all these middle-class white people are getting shoved down to the bottom, where they never thought they'd be. They thought all they had to do was get a college degree and it would be smooth sailing. Maybe they wouldn't be millionaires, but they'd have a house and a car and a boat and two weeks' vacation. Yeah, life would be sweet. Only now that's gone away and they're buzzin' around like a bunch of angry hornets whose hive just got squashed."

"Can you blame them?" I ask.

6 **to fidget** ['fɪdʒɪt] to move nervously – 8 **harrumphs** [hə'rʌmpfs] clears his throat (to show annoyance) – 10 **hood** *(sl)* run down (black) neighborhood in the inner city – 16 **peon** ['piən] *originally* a Spanish-American, now *any*, unskilled worker – 17 **fat cat** *(sl)* very wealthy and influential person – 26 **buzz** the noise a fly or bee makes when in flight; also indicates the moving around – 27 **hornet** *Hornisse* – 27 **hive** [haɪv] structure ("home") in which hornets, bees, wasps etc. live

"Naw, but it's kind of fun to watch. All these folks getting bent out of shape 'cause they ain't getting what they thought they were entitled to."

"I guess when you come down to it, no one's really *entitled* to anything."

Oscar chuckles. "What are you, un-American?"

Knuckles rap on a rear window. I start to turn, but Oscar mutters, "Don't look."

Someone gets into the backseat. The odor of cigarettes and alcohol creeps into the air.

"He cool?" a gravelly voice asks.

"Yeah," Oscar replies, then nods at me. "Go ahead."

Without turning around I explain that I want to know why Aubrey was beaten.

The gravelly voice says, "Because someone wanted it to happen."

"Who?" I ask.

"A guy."

"What guy?" Oscar asks for me.

The voice doesn't answer.

"Go on," Oscar says.

"I don't know. Small guy. Wore a suit."

"You mean, like about a hundred million other small guys in suits?" Oscar asks sardonically.

"Walked with a cane."

My insides involuntarily tighten.

No ... freaking ... way!

"Any other questions?" Oscar asks me.

There have to be, but I'm so shocked by what I've heard that it's hard to think. "Uh, how'd he get to you?"

"A guy named Paul. Used to run sports programs at the youth center."

1 **to be bent out of shape** *here:* annoyed, angry – 3 **entitled to sth** having the right to sth – 7 **knuckle** ['nʌkᵊl] part of the body hand where the fingers join the rest of the hand – 11 **gravelly** rough, harsh – 25 **cane** thin stick that helps sb to walk (thinner than a walking stick)

It hits me like a knock-down pitch. *Dad?* My stomach feels like it wants to turn itself inside out. *It can't be true.* Why would my father help Mr. Purcellen do something like that?

"Any *other* questions?" Oscar asks impatiently.

It's so hard to think. I'm stunned.

"Last chance," Oscar says.

I scramble to make sense of it. Aubrey said the beating was deliberate. "Any idea why the guy in the suit wanted to have my friend's brother beaten up?"

"No," the gravelly voice answers.

A second passes, then the door behind me opens and slams shut.

As soon as Oscar drops me back in Median, I start down the dark sidewalk toward Dignityville. It's after nine now and the demonstration should be over. My brain feels like it's on spin cycle, going around and around but not getting anywhere.

Why would Dad help Mr. Purcellen harm Aubrey?

Ahead I see something that propels me into a jog. Flashing red and blue lights bathe the entrance to Dignityville, and the street is filled with police cars, fire trucks, and media vans. I assume the demonstrators have clashed. But wouldn't that have happened over at Town Hall?

A crowd is milling around in the street in front of the entrance, which is blocked with strips of yellow crime scene tape. A lot of the people outside are Dignityville residents ... the ones who should be *inside.*

I spot Joel. "What's going on?"

"They trashed the place." His voice is high and agitated. "While we were all over at Town Hall."

"Who's 'they'?"

"Don't know."

1 **knock-down punch** when you are hit with sb's fist and knocked out unconscious – 7 **scramble** struggle – 23 **to mill around** to move around in a random, unordered way

"Have you seen my parents?"

"Not since the demonstration."

Murmurs spread through the crowd and heads turn. A group of men comes out of Dignityville–the chief of police and the mayor, followed by Dad, Wade, and a few others. Looking glum, Mayor George stops at the yellow tape. Video cam beams form a spotlight. The media crowds in.

"I'll make a brief statement," the mayor announces somberly, then waits for everyone to quiet down. "I've just had a tour of what remains of Dignityville. The damage has been extensive and it's clear that this was not a random act of vandalism. Whoever did it specifically targeted those things that will be most difficult to replace–the washing area, the outdoor heaters, and the television. In addition many of the tents were slashed and damaged."

"Any clues as to who did it?" asks a reporter.

"Not at the moment. The investigation is just beginning."

"What about a motive?"

"It's pretty obvious that whoever did this wanted to make sure that Dignityville would be unfit for habitation."

"What'll happen to the residents?"

Mayor George tugs at his earlobe. "That's what we have to figure out right now." The interview ends and he heads quickly toward a waiting car. Dad stays behind, talking to Wade and our neighbors Fred and Diane. Diane's sobbing. Dad puts his arm around her shoulders and comforts her.

Does any of this make sense?

A hand touches my arm. It's Mom, looking upset. "Where have you been? We've been worried sick about you."

"I'm okay. What about Meg's dad?"

"They took him and a few others to the hospital."

"Was he hurt?" It's horrible to think they'd do that to someone so ill.

"I haven't heard of anyone being hurt," Mom says. "But I was so worried about *you*. We had no idea where you were."

"There you are." Dad joins us. "Where were you?"

My eyes meet his. I don't know what to say to him. He looks at the ground and shakes his head. "Can you believe it?"

If only you knew. …

Do I tell him what I know?

Do I ask him why he did it?

Not now. The most important thing right now is to help figure out where people will stay tonight, and what will happen tomorrow.

I will ask him … when the time is right.

The police say it's not safe to go into Dignityville tonight. Around the entrance there's confusion. People are upset. They want to know what's happened to their things. They need their medicine. I look for Meg, but don't see her. I suspect she and her mom are at the hospital with Mr. Fine and Aubrey.

Gradually the crowd settles down on the curb to wait. It never occurred to me that there could be another step down from Dignityville. But there is–the street.

Hours pass while things get sorted out. Dad leads a group of us to Saint Stephen's, the site of the near food fight the night we cooked chili. They've set up cots in the basement. Almost instantly there are long lines for the two bathrooms we'll all have to use. We're starting to settle in when Mayor George, collar askew and looking haggard, stops by to tell us that tomorrow we can go back to Dignityville to get our things. People pepper him with questions: Who did it? Why? Where will the homeless go now? Mayor George has no answers.

20 **cot** *(AE)* portable bed – 23 **askew** [ə'skjuː] not straight – 23 **haggard** very tired or fed up

38

No one gets more than a few hours of rest. The next morning my fuzzy, sleep-deprived brain can't seem to process nuance or transition. Two nights ago hunger kept me from getting a decent night's sleep, but I managed to power through yesterday on adrenaline. Now, after a second sleepless night, the adrenaline's dissipated and my thoughts have a fragmented quality. Life feels more like the separate slides of a PowerPoint presentation than a continuous live-action movie.

Outside it's cold and rainy, a truly crappy day to spend cleaning up a decimated camp for homeless people. I want to get Dad alone and talk to him. I want to help at Dignityville, but Mom tells me to go to school.

In the hall my sleep-deprived brain feels like it's lagging ten feet behind the rest of me. I look for Meg, but it's not unusual for me to go a whole morning and not see her. As lunchtime approaches, in addition to dazed and wobbly, I start to feel apprehensive. Talia will be there. How do I face her, knowing what I know about her father? Knowing what I know about *my* father?

In the kitchen Lisa the lunch lady's lips wrinkle sadly. "You okay, honey?"

No. I am so far from okay that I'm not even sure what the word means anymore.

But I shrug. "Guess so." Then, because I don't want to appear so gloomy, I force a smile. "We're still here, right?"

Lisa smiles back. "That's what counts."

Does it?

I feel my pulse accelerate when I get my first look at the table. Noah and Tory are there, but Talia isn't. Then I remember she said she and her mom were flying to the Northeast for a long

6 **to dissipate** to go away – 16 **dazed** mentally confused – 16 **wobbly** unsteady, shaking – 17 **apprehensive** uneasy, fearful of the future

weekend looking at colleges. That's a relief. At least I won't have to deal with the supreme awkwardness of facing her.

As I approach the table, the conversation softens to a whisper, then dies. Even though I know it's because they don't want to hurt my feelings, it still reminds me that I'm no longer part of their world. Today I can't even pretend that Dignityville is my home. I'm the only one at the table who isn't sure where he's sleeping tonight, or when he'll have his next meal. I know they'll all continue to be generous and kind, but I can't help thinking of Blanche DuBois and what she said about depending on the kindness of strangers. My friends have become strangers.

Noah stares at my shirt. With a jolt I realize why: I'm wearing the same clothes I wore yesterday … and slept in last night. The others must realize it too, because I feel them trying not to look. It's unbelievable. I've gotten to the point where I make my own friends uncomfortable.

"Know what today is?" Noah finally asks, trying to sound cheerful.

I peer at him blankly. *What can today possibly be?*

He gives me a concerned look. "Two weeks until the Fall Classic … but listen, if you want to take a couple of days off?"

I can't take more days off. Not if I want to be outstanding at the tournament. Not if I want to hold on to the only hope left for getting me and my family out of this mess. "I'll be there this afternoon."

Up goes a skeptical eyebrow. "You sure?"

"A man got to do what he got to do." Rarely have those words felt as hollow as they do right now.

Noah nods uncertainly. "Okay, then. This is the final stretch. For the next two weeks we bump it up another notch."

Two weeks … and I'm not even sure where I'll be living then.

By the time school ends I'm having trouble walking a straight line. My body doesn't want to practice; it wants to lie down in

30 **to bump up** to raise, to increase – 30 **notch** *(inf)* level

the hallway and go to sleep. But I can't. I owe it to Noah to be there. I owe it to my parents.

It's too cold and wet to go outside, so we use the indoor pitching mound in the gym.

A few miles away a bunch of homeless people have no choice but to be out in that cold and wet with no real idea of where they're sleeping tonight.

Because Mr. Purcellen is worried about the value of his real estate.

The pitching mound is ten and a half inches high, made of AstroTurf, and slopes down in front. Standing on it, I rub a ball in my hands, feeling the seams and tiny irregularities in the scuffed surface that will make it fly through the air with its own unique path. And just as every baseball is slightly different, so is every human being. And like every pitch, every human will follow its own unique path.

To where?

Wearing his mask and chest protector, Noah squats down roughly sixty-two feet away. Above us the gym's big duct fans whir and the halide lights hum.

"Ready," he calls.

The ball feels rough in spots. Practice balls get scuffed. Life is about getting scuffed. The older we are, the more scuffed we get. Only some of us get scuffed more and sooner than others.

I'm so tired I swear I could close my eyes and go to sleep standing up.

"Ready?" Noah repeats.

Feeling light-headed, I put my foot on the rubber and look down at the ball in my hand. The red stitching, the cowhide. The game I've played my whole life. Above me the whirring fans grow louder and the lights seem brighter.

11 **Astro Turf** trademark for artificial grass used on sports grounds *(Kunstrasen)* – 12 **seam** line where two pieces of material have been stitched together – 13 **scuffed** scratched – 19 **duct fan** air cooling machine with rotating blades in a tube – 20 **halide** *halogen* – 29 **cowhide** *(AE)* cow's skin (so: leather)

"Ready!"

With the ball nestled inside it, I lift my mitt in front of my face, and stare at Noah for the sign.

He starts to signal fastball.

Then he rises out of sight and gets replaced by something green.

It's the AstroTurf, rushing toward me.

"Dan?" a voice calls from far away.

I open my eyes. Dark shapes hover against a bright background. "Dan?"

I'm lying on my back. The shapes come into focus: Noah … Coach Buder … Zach … Tyler …

My face hurts. The floor under my back feels hard. Zach and Tyler are each holding one of my ankles so that my legs angle upward. "What happened?" I ask.

"You fainted."

The pain in my face starts to localize to my right eye and one of my front teeth.

"How do you feel?" Buddha asks.

"Not sure."

"Help him sit up."

Hands prop me into a sitting position. My right eye throbs and it's hard to see out of it. With the tip of my tongue, I feel a small gap where part of a tooth used to be. Buddha gives me a concerned look, but Noah, still wearing his chest protector, seems to be fighting off a grin.

"What's so funny?"

"You look like someone kicked the crap out of you."

"Try to get up?" Buddha asks.

"Okay." Fainting isn't a big deal. Guys get woozy and keel over now and then, especially during long practices on hot days. It's

16 **to faint** to lose consciousness – 28 **to kick the crap out of sb** *(inf)* to hit sb violently; beat sb up – 30 **woozy** disoriented – 30 **to keel over** to collapse

happened to me a few times before, but usually on a grassy field where it doesn't hurt as much.

The guys get me up to my feet, where for a moment I feel light-headed, but this time I bend over with my hands on my thighs and get my head down around knee level. Hands steady me while the blood rushes back to my brain.

When I slowly straighten up, the dizziness is mostly gone. Buddha, who's seen this happen dozens of times, studies me. "Think you're all right?"

"Yeah."

He turns to the others. "Get him into the locker room and we'll put a cold pack on that eye."

Noah and Zach keep their hands on my elbows as they escort me into the locker room. When we pass a mirror, I catch a glimpse of myself with a swollen, black-and-blue eye, and a puffy, split lip. I pull my lips back and there's a triangular gap where one of my front teeth has broken on the diagonal.

Great, now I'm one step closer to becoming one of those old, toothless guys at Dignityville.

Buddha arrives with a cold pack and I press it gingerly against my eye. Noah tells me how I swayed for a moment, then fell face-first off the mound, the mitt with the ball exactly at eye level.

When they see that I'm okay, the others gradually drift away, but Noah stays until I'm ready to leave. "Where are we going?" he asks in the car.

"Not sure," I answer, still holding the cold pack to my eye. "Try Saint Stephen's."

As we head into town, Noah says, "I hate to say this, man, but maybe you've got too much going on right now to be worried about that tournament?"

"Maybe," I have to admit.

7 **dizziness** feeling that you are about to fall – 21 **to sway** to swing to and fro

"I mean, think about it. There's something like thirty thousand high schools in this country, and most teams have at least three or four pitchers. And that's not counting the Dominican Republic, Puerto Rico, and Canada. So how many real eighteen-year-old prospects are out there? A thousand? And how many actually get drafted out of high school each year?"

We both know the answer. "About twenty."

"The phenoms," Noah says. He doesn't have to add what we already know: I may be a good pitcher, maybe even *really* good, but a phenom? It's doubtful.

"So what am I gonna do?" I ask, trying to resist the defeated sensation that threatens to close in.

"Finish school, go to college."

"And my parents?"

Noah scratches his temple as he steers. "Honestly?"

"Yeah."

"It's not like they're sick or can't take care of themselves, Dan. Maybe, right now, they're not your problem."

5 **prospect** *here:* candidate (prospective pro player) – 6 **drafted** selected – 8 **phenom** *(inf)* person of outstanding abilities (*abb* for **phenomenal player**)

39

Our new home is the Route 7 Motor Inn, a decrepit motel beside a busy highway. Mom and Dad have salvaged what they could from Dignityville and we were moved here by social services. We're in one room with two sagging twin beds. The air stinks of antiseptic and the stale memory of cigarette smoke, and there are dark cigarette burns on the dresser and windowsill. Sunlight seeps in around the heavy curtains. From outside comes the steady rumble of trucks and cars on Route 7.

Despite the smells and noises, I sleep for something like fourteen hours. My parents weren't there when I crawled into bed around seven p.m. last night, but this morning when I wake, Mom asks about the black eye and broken tooth. I tell her I got hit by a pitch in batting practice. Dad gives me a dubious look, but doesn't pursue it. Mom says I'll have to go to the dentist about the tooth.

Do dentists take food stamps?

There's hardly enough space in this room for the three of us and our unpacked bags. It's Saturday and this is my chance to talk to Dad about Aubrey's beating and Mr. Purcellen, but my gut tells me not to say anything in front of Mom. Now and then his and my eyes meet and it's obvious that he knows I want to talk. And also obvious that he's not real thrilled about it. But there are other questions I can ask: "What happens to Dignityville?"

Dad slowly shakes his head. "It's over. Everyone's in shelters and welfare motels like this. Back where they were before there ever was a Dignityville."

"What does Mayor George say?" I ask.

"That it was a worthy experiment," Dad answers. "What he doesn't say is that it's a win for the local landowners. Thanks to them the homeless are invisible again."

1 **decrepit** [dɪˈkrepɪt] run down – 2 **salvaged** saved for further use

Mom pulls the curtain back to reveal the parking lot, and beyond it, the highway. Tears roll down her cheeks. Dad gets up and puts his arms around her. "Don't worry, we won't be here long."

Her forehead wrinkles as she wipes the tears away with the back of her hand. "How can you say that?"

Dad shoots me a "don't question this" look, then says, "Just believe me."

40

I spend the rest of the weekend doing homework, watching TV, catching up on sleep, waiting for a chance to get Dad alone. Mom's gotten a pay-as-you-go phone, and I speak to Noah and tell him I'm okay. I guess I'm lucky that Talia's away looking at schools. On Sunday night we go to Uncle Ron's for dinner again. He no longer acts angry, or disdainful of Dad. If anything, he seems puzzled, as if he can't understand what's happened to us.

On Monday morning a hand shakes my shoulder and my eyes open into Mom's face. The motel room is dim, light filtering around the curtains. The din of traffic seeps in. "Hurry, sweetheart," she whispers. "The bus is here."

What bus?

"I'll try to get them to wait." She hustles out the motel room door.

It seems too early for a school bus, but I pull on whatever clothes are lying around, try to shake the cobwebs out of my brain, grab my books. Dad's still asleep.

Outside the chill hits. It's been a mild fall up till now, but this morning there's frost on the windows of the cars parked outside the motel. My breath clouds and my broken tooth throbs when I inhale the brisk air. A school van idles at the curb and Mom stands beside the closed door, hugging herself in the cold. Young faces in the van windows peer out at me.

The door opens. As I pass Mom, she gives me a kiss on the cheek. A few years ago a kiss from Mom before boarding a school bus would have scored an eleven on the embarrassment scale of ten, but what difference does it make now? I've just come out of a run-down motel with a black eye and a broken tooth. Once again it's hard to imagine sinking much lower.

6 **disdainful** rude, insulting – 16 **cobwebs** *(pl)* confusion, disorder *(usu: Spinnennetz)* – 20 **to throb** to hurt

Inside, the kids are all ages–elementary, middle, and high school. With only a few seats left, I take one next to a little kid. Gradually waking up, I glance around at my bus mates and notice little things: the frayed hems of their jeans, the worn heals of their sneakers, the holes in the elbows of their hoodies.

The van stops at another crappy motel a few blocks away, and four more kids climb on. There aren't enough seats, and two of them have to stand in the back even though I thought that's not allowed on school buses. But this is no ordinary early-morning, long-distance van picking up kids from the hinterlands. This … is the Homeless Kid Express.

***

When we get to school half an hour before the first bell, I realize it's because it's assumed that all of us qualify for free breakfasts. Inside the building an envelope is taped to my locker with a note from Ms. Reuben inviting me to stop by her office and chat if I feel like it.

If I do, I wonder what free stuff I can get this time. …

Whoa … I can't believe I just thought that.

Welcome to How to Think Like a Homeless Person.

I hang up my jacket, dump some books, and with my stomach grumbling and nothing to do until school starts, give in to hunger and head toward the cafeteria to see what I can scrounge up. Yeah, I know I'm the one who said I'd never stoop to a free breakfast.

Most of the kids from the Homeless Kid Express are down there, along with a bunch of others, including Meg. I never officially signed up for free breakfasts, but Lisa's in the kitchen and without a word I get milk, a whole-wheat donut, and a bowl of Lucky Charms.

When I sit down opposite Meg, her eyes widen with concern. "What happened to you?"

4 **frayed hems** *ausgefranste Säume* – 5 **hoodie** sweatshirt with a part that covers your head – 24 **to stoop to** *(here)* to accept sth that you would not normally take

I'm tempted to go with the old "If you think this is bad, you should see the other guy" joke, but she might think it had something to do with the demonstration. So instead I tell her the truth, then ask, "What about you? Where're you staying?"

"Dad's at the hospital because there's no place for him to go right now. He has no idea that Aubrey's there. They put Mom and me in a women's shelter. What about you?"

I tell her about the welfare motel. "My father says we won't be there for long. It's just hard to imagine where else we can go. So … does Aubrey know what happened?"

Meg nods sadly. "He's so disappointed. And you know what's strange? In a way I almost miss Dignityville now."

As lunchtime nears, I feel myself growing tight and anxious at the prospect of seeing Talia. In the cafeteria her expression compresses when she sees me. "What happened to your face?"

The table goes quiet. They're all trying not to stare, probably thinking that this is the sort of thing that happens to the homeless. More evidence that life is rough out there in the world of the disadvantaged. But guys don't like to admit that they fainted, so I need to come up with something. And it's going to be a double whammy, because as soon as I answer, she's going to see my chipped tooth. "I had an accident."

"In a car?" she asks.

"On an indoor baseball mound."

"Pushing himself too hard." Noah comes to my aid, trying to make it sound heroic. And then, to take the focus off me, he asks Talia about the schools she visited over the weekend.

When Talia tells us about Sarah Lawrence, Skidmore, Smith, and Swarthmore, I can't help wondering if she's arranged her college visits alphabetically. She talks about how beautiful the

21 **double whammy** two setbacks in one – 22 **chipped** broken – 28 **Sarah Lawrence** exclusive private college 15 miles north of Manhattan – 28 **Skidmore** private college in New York State – 29 **Swarthmore** private college in Swarthmore, Pennsylvania

campuses are and how she wishes she and her mom could have visited a few weeks ago when the fall colors were at their peak. It's pretty obvious that she doesn't want to talk about my new "situation," at least not in front of her friends. And of course she can't possibly have the slightest clue about her father's involvement in the trashing of Dignityville.

Two squares of pizza lay untouched on my lunch tray. It's hard to find an appetite when you're so tightly wound up, but I force myself to pick a piece up and take a bite.

Just in case this is my last meal of the day.

I haven't given up on the Thanksgiving tournament, but Noah hasn't said anything about practicing today, which is fine because it's driving me crazy that I still haven't spoken to Dad. After school I catch the Homeless Kid Express back to the End of the World Motel. The dimly lit room smells of incense, and Mom's sitting on her bed, a book beside her. But I get the feeling she hasn't been reading.

"Been here all day?" I ask.

She shrugs, nods.

"Where's Dad?"

"He had some business to attend to."

I can just imagine. ... Wait, actually, I can't. That's what's so frustrating.

"Come on." I hold the door open, allowing the sunlight and air in.

"Where?" Mom asks.

"I don't know. Anyplace but here."

She pulls on a sweater and shoes and we step around the potholes in the parking lot. The air is foul with car and truck exhaust and the clamor of engines. Across the highway are some gas stations, a pawn shop, and a junkyard surrounded by a tall metal fence.

5 **clue** idea, information – 29 **pothole** large hole in the surface of a road – 30 **exhaust** [ɪɡˈzɑːst] the smoke that comes out of a motor vehicle as waste gas

Not a patch of green in sight.

This corner of the world hardly feels fit for human habitation. Given where we've wound up, I wonder if Mom would prefer to be back in the negative energy of Uncle Ron's, but I don't ask. If she wanted to go back there, she'd say so.

We stand on the curb and look around forlornly. I'd hoped we'd take a walk, but to where? No direction looks promising. There's nothing in the distance to fix one's hopes to. The phrase "no direction home" comes to mind, although I don't know how I know it or where I heard it.

I feel Mom's eyes, as if she's waiting for me to decide which way to go.

Far down the street a U-Haul van turns a corner and starts toward us. There's no reason to pay attention to it. No reason why it should mean more than any other van. Maybe I watch it because it reminds me of the day we lost our house, the day the Great Pitch Count of Life started to go against us.

The van grows bigger as the distance decreases. I keep waiting for it to turn a corner and disappear.

Strangely, it comes closer and closer until it stops at the light on the other side of Route 7. I can't see who's driving through the tinted windshield.

The light turns green, and the van crosses the highway and pulls into the motel parking lot.

The driver is Dad.

6 **forlornly** hopelessly, desperately – 17 **Pitch Count** *here:* fate (refers to counting the number of pitches a pitcher throws in baseball. The idea is that sb is watching them.)

41

We're moving, but Dad won't tell us where–says he wants it to be a surprise. But he's quiet and moody and hardly seems happy about it himself. Neither Mom nor I press him, maybe because we both know that wherever we're headed can't be worse than where we've been. With the three of us squeezed into the front seat, it again feels like we're the Joads, just another Okie family being swept along by forces beyond our control.

A short while later we pull into a fragment of a neighborhood where only a few houses have been completed and a handful more appear to have been started and then abandoned–wooden frameworks and muddy front yards littered with construction debris. The rest of the landscape is unfinished driveways leading to empty lots choked with tall weeds.

Dad parks the van in the driveway of one of the finished houses–two stories high, painted gray-blue, with a red door. In the front yard a few patches of long grass struggle to survive–the remnants of what was once a lawn.

"What's going on?" Mom asks.

"Our new home," Dad says in a flat voice, and starts to get out. "Come on, we've got work to do."

He goes around behind the van. Mom and I stay in the front seat.

"Did you know about this?" I ask.

She shakes her head.

"Hey," Dad calls from the back. "I can't do it alone."

In the back are boxes and the few pieces of unsold furniture we'd put in storage months ago–stuff Dad wouldn't have taken out unless we were moving somewhere for a long time.

"How is this possible?" Mom asks.

6 **Joads** fictional migrant family in *The Grapes of Wrath* – 6 **Okie** derogatory word for migrant workers from Oklahoma in the 1930s – 11 **muddy** dirty with wet earth – 12 **debris** *(pl)* litter – 13 **choked** covered – 13 **weed** wild plant – 17 **the remnants** *(pl n)* what is left over after sth has been used (or, as here, harmed)

"I'll tell you later," Dad answers in his "not in front of Dan" voice.

Mom frowns, but accepts this. Avoiding my eyes, Dad hands me a folding table. But when Mom steps up to take something, he manages a weak smile. "Hey, why don't you go check out the backyard?"

She gives him a quizzical look, but goes. Before I can say anything, Dad grabs a box and turns toward the house, almost as if he's trying to avoid me. I follow, carrying the table up the front walk. Inside, the living room is empty, floors bare, no shades on the windows, wires dangling from the ceiling where light fixtures should go. It looks like no one's ever lived here.

We lug our things into the kitchen. The faucet's missing and the tags are still on the refrigerator. Through the window we see Mom outside, surveying the backyard.

"Dad?"

"Don't ask."

"I *have* to."

His shoulders sag as our eyes meet. He doesn't look away, the way someone who's ashamed of what he's done might. He nods at Mom outside, then looks straight at me as if trying to say, *Whatever I did, I did for you and Mom.*

"That time I saw you get out of Mr. Purcellen's pickup ...," I begin.

Now he looks away.

I gesture around the kitchen. "Is this why you put him in touch with that gang?"

He jerks his head back and stares up at me with eyes as wide as catcher's mitts. "How do you ...?" he starts, then trails off, clearly stunned.

I tell him what I learned that night in the Range Rover. "Why would Talia's father come to you?"

10 **bare** [ber] naked – 13 **to lug** *(inf)* to carry sth with difficulty – 13 **faucet** ['fɑːsɪt] *(AE)* *Wasserhahn* – 14 **(price) tag** piece of paper telling you the price of sth – 30 **stunned** astonished

He lets out a long sigh. "He knew I had connections to the kind of people he needed."

"You knew what they were going to do to Aubrey?"

"God, no." He shakes his head vehemently. "They weren't supposed to hurt him, just get him to stop trying to make Dignityville permanent."

"So why didn't you go to the police?"

There in the empty kitchen, Dad tells me the whole story of how he stupidly agreed to help Mr. Purcellen in exchange for a place to live, and how, after Aubrey was beaten, Talia's father strong-armed him into staying quiet by threatening to tell me what had happened. He blinks hard. "I couldn't let you find out. I already felt like enough of a failure."

"What about ransacking Dignityville?" I ask. "How'd he get you to organize the demonstration?"

Dad runs a finger across the counter, leaving a stripe in the dust. "He said he knew people ... wealthy donors to Rice ... who could stop you from getting a scholarship if I didn't cooperate. I don't know if it was true, but I couldn't take a chance. And I was afraid people would be hurt if I didn't get them out of there." His eyes glisten with tears of shame and regret. "After what happened to Aubrey ..." He wipes his eyes with the back of his hand.

Whatever he did, he did for Mom and me.

A man got to do what he got to do.

But what if what he does is wrong?

The back door opens and Mom comes in, throws her arms around Dad and hugs him, burying her face against his chest, not noticing that he's got tears in his eyes. "It's ... wonderful! Oh, thank you, darling, I have a garden again!"

For a moment they hug, but then, still holding him close, she whispers, "But how, Paul? You have to tell me."

11 **to strong-arm** to force – 14 **to ransack** to go through a place, stealing things and causing damage; to plunder – 17 **donor** ['doʊnɚ] person who contributes money to an institution

It's Dad's turn to give *me* the "Don't say anything in front of Mom" look.

"If they want to sell these houses, they need to make it look like people are already living here," he says. "We're the decoy that encourages the other ducks to land."

"How long will they let us stay?" she asks.

"Long enough."

For now Mom has no more questions. Dad gazes over her shoulder at me with red-rimmed eyes. He knows what he did was wrong, but it was done out of love and desperation. It was the act of a man who believed he was a failure, and had nothing left to lose.

4 **decoy** sth that is used to attract or distract sb *(Lockvogel)*

42

No one's parents are perfect.

Some fathers have bad judgment.

Some lose their tempers.

Some can't seem to hold a job or be successful at work.

Some mothers think they're supposed to be successful at work. And then change their minds.

But most parents try to do the right things for their families and communities.

Most, but not all.

In an office in the Median Police Department with Detective French and an assistant district attorney, Dad finishes telling his story.

"So when you put Purcellen in touch with that gang, you had no idea what he was planning?" the assistant district attorney asks.

Dad shakes his head.

"You didn't wonder?"

"I did. I asked, but he told me it was none of my business." Dad hangs his head. "It was a mistake. I never should have done it."

"Bad judgment isn't a crime, Mr. Halprin," the assistant district attorney says. "If it was, we'd all have criminal records." He stands up, says he'll be in touch, then leaves.

"Now what?" I ask Detective French.

"We'll investigate." She rises from her desk and offers her hand. Dad and I shake it and he heads for the door. I let him go ahead–" I'll catch up in a second, Dad"–then turn back to Detective French. Our eyes meet and I give her a questioning look. She remembers that day we spoke in Starbucks because I mentioned it when I first told her that Dad wanted to speak to her about Aubrey's beating.

3 **to lose one's temper** to become very angry

"We'll contact the Burlington police," she says. "It's their jurisdiction. But, Dan, keep in mind that gangbangers have a way of vanishing when word hits the street that the police are looking for them."

In other words, I shouldn't hold my breath.

"What about the house Mr. Purcellen gave us?" I ask. "Isn't that evidence?"

"I imagine Mr. Purcellen's lawyers will claim you were squatters who had no right to move in," she replies. "It's your father's word against his, Dan. Unless we can find witnesses or develop corroborating evidence, there's very little ..."

She continues talking, but I've tuned out. It's not her fault. I know that if she had the time and resources to build a case, she would. Not just because it's her job, but because she believes in justice. But now that we live in the United States of Part-Time Law Enforcement, there's only so much justice to go around.

8 **squatter** sb who lives in a building without paying rent or owning it – 11 **corroborating evidence** additional facts that show that sth is true – 12 **to tune out** *(inf)* to stop paying attention

43

In *The Grapes of Wrath* homelessness meant being on the move. When the Joads got to California, they lived in Hooverville, then Weedpatch, then a boxcar, until the rains brought flooding. At the end of the book they were moving again, this time in search of higher, drier ground.

I'm amazed at how calm Mom is after Dad takes her for a walk and tells her the story. Maybe she's just used to him messing up, and knows that he only did what he did for our sakes. Still, she says we can't stay in that house, garden or no garden. We've barely unpacked, so our stuff goes back into storage. When I call Mason and explain we have nowhere to go that night, his parents say we can stay in the apartment above their garage.

Dealing with Talia turns out to be a nonissue. She's aghast at the story her father told her of how my father tried to blackmail him into giving us a house by threatening to blame him for the ransacking of Dignityville. In fact, Mr. Purcellen would have gone to the police had Talia not begged him to reconsider. But now that Talia accepts "the truth," she doesn't know how we can continue to see each other.

For an instant I'm tempted to tell her the other side of the story, but then I remember what Detective French said: It's her father's word against mine. And besides, it's over between Talia and me. I'm finished pretending.

More than half a million people march on Washington over Thanksgiving to protest financial inequality in this country, and millions more attend rallies in towns and cities all over. I pitch in the Fall Classic. Pro scouts are there and I hear later that a

7 **to mess up** *(inf)* to do sth wrong, make a mistake – 13 **nonissue** matter of no importance – 13 **aghast** [ə'gæst] shocked

couple of players actually do get draft offers. I guess they're the phenoms. But at least the scouts see me, and a few say I show promise and they'll keep an eye on me.

So maybe … in a couple of years … if I keep working hard and improving …

I wish I could say that the police were able to connect Mr. Purcellen to Aubrey's beating and what happened to Dignityville, but that hasn't happened … yet. There have been rumors, though, and those alone must hurt. Sometimes in the hall Talia looks pale and glum. I feel bad for her.

***

It's basketball season now. The trees are bare and every morning there's frost on the ground around Mason's house. Dad's getting lots of little jobs reffing games after school and at night. They don't pay a lot, but the games are short, and sometimes on a weekend he can work three or four of them a day. Mom has a job cooking in a vegan restaurant. I'm a little nervous that she's going to insist on going vegan at home, but so far she hasn't.

I signed the letter of intent with Rice, so that's all set for next year. And I'm working a few evenings a week and weekends as a busboy at Ruby's so I can save some money between now and then. Noah and I hang out when we can, but it's awkward with Talia being Tory's best friend. It's just as well. They can make whatever plans they want now without having to be concerned with whether I can afford to join them.

Meg's dad is in a hospice. She says he doesn't have much time left. I've been hanging out with her a lot; we're definitely beyond friends. Sometimes I toss a tennis ball with Aubrey to help him get his hand-eye coordination back. He's already talking about starting another Dignityville on private land so no town money has to be involved.

19 **letter of intent** written statement expressing the writer's intention of doing sth

In the meantime the Fines will be moving into a Habitat for Humanity house that was donated to the town after Dignityville was destroyed. The owners of the house said that before Dignityville they'd had no idea how many people in Median were homeless.

I've heard that some other houses were donated as well.

So I guess some good came out of Mayor George's "worthy experiment" after all.

EPILOGUE

It's too bad that the baseball tournament had to be on the same weekend as the march, but I still think I made the right choice. For me.

There are people like Martin Luther King Jr., Mahatma Gandhi, Rosa Parks, Nelson Mandela, and maybe even Aubrey Fine, who somehow know they're meant to change things in a big way. I don't know how they know it, but they do.

On the bus coming back from the tournament, I found another quote in *The Grapes of Wrath*:

> Wherever they's a fight so hungry people can eat, I'll be there. Wherever they's a cop beatin' up a guy, I'll be there. ... I'll be in the way guys yell when they're mad–an' I'll be in the way kids laugh when they're hungry an' they know supper's ready. An' when our folks eat the stuff they raise an' live in the houses they build–why, I'll be there.

Some things have changed since the Great Depression–the police are here to protect the homeless and the people who strike for better pay, not to beat them up.

But it's weird how a lot of things haven't changed. Nearly a third of our country is living at or near the poverty level, and on the news we keep hearing that homelessness and unemployment are close to the highest they've been since the Depression. Some people still go hungry, and many can't afford medical care.

I just can't help thinking about how *The Grapes of Wrath* is based on events that happened nearly a hundred years ago.

How is it possible that so many of the problems people faced back then are still the problems we face today?

Acknowledgments

My thanks to Coach Michael Chiapparelli and pitcher Michael Williams for their gracious assistance.

And to David Gale, Navah Wolfe, and Dr. Petra Deistler-Kaufmann, for their many insightful and helpful suggestions.

Additional texts: Todd Strasser

1. Interview

2. Extract from a lecture, 2015

1. Interview with Todd Strasser, conducted by the editor of this edition, Peter Bruck

This interview was conducted especially for this edition in November 2019.

PB: *The financial crisis of 2008, in which many people lost their mortgaged homes, obviously played a role in the writing of this book. What kind of research did you do for it? Did you visit any actual tent camps?*

TS: I was able to visit tent camps in California, where the problem of homelessness increased dramatically in the past decade despite a much-improved economy. The problem in our country is no longer that of people losing their homes, but that people cannot afford to buy a home. In addition, I did a lot of research, relying on news reports, and speaking to people familiar with such camps.

PB: *You also made a series of photographs of various tents housing homeless people. What was your most meaningful or emotional experience?*

TS: Coming across an unconscious homeless man who had soiled himself. He was lying facedown in a parking lot, surrounded by empty beer cans.

PB: *Compared to shacks and real tent cities, Dignityville is a fairly comfortable place. I wonder why you chose to describe it in this way?*

6 **mortgaged** ['mɔːrgidʒd] *(adj)* owned by the bank, but the people who use the building are repaying – 10 **decade** 10 years – 20 **to soil oneself** *sich besudeln*

TS: The characters in the book are mostly responsible, mostly hard-working, mostly wishing to improve their lot in life. They had not given up. I felt that Dignityville was the sort of place they would most likely seek out.

PB: *Your narrator Dan Halpin describes his observations and events in a somewhat detached manner. This is quite surprising given the dramatic changes in his life. Why did you make him narrate in this way?*

TS: I think Dan's detachment reflects his inability to truly accept his family's circumstances.

PB: *To my mind Dan is the only character that develops throughout the action, whereas the others – Meg, Talia, Noah etc. – seem to be stock characters. What effect did you wish to create by that?*

TS: That is certainly Dan's perception of them. They are foils for the purpose of contrast.

PB: *Towards the end, the novel takes an optimistic tone. The Halpins live in an apartment, they have jobs and even the Fines can move into a house that was donated to homeless people. Did you want to re-establish American optimism here?*

TS: Ha! Well, I suppose so, although I'm not certain how optimistic Americans are these days about the state of our country. But also because the book is written for young people and I wanted to have a positive end.

2 **lot** *here:* situation – 6 **detached** [dɪˈtætʃt] distanced, dry – 15 **foil** opposite (*usu* related to a character in a book, film or play)

PB: *Occasionally there are didactic passages in which economic problems, the effects of globalization, etc. are explained to the reader. Is there a particular social or political position in the novel that you wanted to show?*

TS: Because it's a topic that would be foreign to many young American readers, I did feel things had to be spelled out clearly. I do wish that the US would become more of a social democracy.

PB: *The novel abounds with references to Steinbeck's* The Grapes of Wrath. *The very fact that the Halpins are better off than the Joads might suggest that the homeless of today live in better circumstances than those of the Great Depression. Do you go along with that? What are the similarities and/or differences between the two situations, do you think?*

TS: In some cases, yes. There is more help for those homeless people who ask for help or seek it out. But sadly, many do not seem to want any help. The homeless today often, though not always, have access to some level of organized healthcare. There are laws designed to protect them. There are numerous programs dedicated to trying to help them. But for a variety of reasons, some of the homeless do not want help.

17 **access** ['ækses] *Zugang*

2. Homelessness: From a lecture by Todd Strasser

"Today, the unemployment rate is the lowest it's been in decades. But unlike what I imagine life was like after the great depression, today homelessness still persists. In 2009, nearly 1.5 million people in this country were homeless. That number has indeed dropped since the great recession, but still on any given day in this country there are nearly half a million people who are homeless. And over the course of any given year, close to three and a half million will find themselves at least temporarily without a place to live. I live near New York City and recently I was shocked to read in *The New York Times* that at any given moment nearly ten per cent of public school students in the city are either living with their families in shelters, or with relatives. In other words, one in ten public school students in New York City – surely one of the wealthiest cities in the world – will be homeless at some point during the year. [...]

"There are many reasons why people are homeless. Approximately twenty percent, or one in five, are said to be homeless because of mental issues and/or drug abuse. But if they represent only 20 percent of the total homeless population in this country, then who are the others? And why are they homeless?

"One reason is still unemployment. If you're living paycheck to paycheck with very little savings and you lose your job, you can become homeless very quickly. Again, referring to *The New York Times*, the persistent level of homelessness today may reflect a growing divide within the American workforce. Despite increasing numbers of well-paying jobs in the tech industry, the *Times* article stated that "the vast majority of new jobs are still in workaday service industries, like health care, hospitality, retail

23 **to live paycheck to paycheck** when you are using most or all of your monthly income to cover your monthly expenses – with no money left over and no money in savings – 27 **American workforce** all the people that work in America – 30 **workaday** common, ordinary – 30 **hospitality** jobs where you have to welcome people (e.g. hotels) – 30 **retail** selling of goods to consumers

and building services, where the pay is mediocre." The article goes on to say: "Automation is changing the nature of work, flushing workers without a college degree out of productive industries like manufacturing and high-tech services and into tasks with meager wages and no prospect for advancing. [...]

"Health emergencies also cause homelessness. It could be a health problem that affects you, or someone you care about. Not everyone has health insurance and even those who have it are liable to find that it doesn't cover all of their medical expenses. People with cancer for instance – regardless of whether or not they have health insurance – are nearly three times more likely to declare bankruptcy than healthy people. Nearly 60 percent of all personal bankruptcies in this country are the result of unaffordable medical bills.

"Yet another factor leading to homelessness is lack of affordable housing. As you know, the rents in cities like San Francisco and New York are ludicrous. But even outside these urban areas, people are feeling crunched by the rising cost of living. I've read that this is an issue right here in Riverside County as well. According to the Department of Housing and Urban Development, families with only one full-time worker on the minimum wage cannot afford to rent a two-bedroom apartment anywhere in this country. [...]"

1 **mediocre** [ˌmiːdiˈoʊkɚ] barely adequate, poor – 3 **to flush sb out ... and into** make sb leave one job and enter another – 5 **meager** [ˈmiːgɚ] minimal – 17 **ludicrous** ridiculous (*here:* very expensive) – 18 **crunched** squeezed by financial pressure